REMEMBRANCE OF LOVE
AND OTHER CAPE BRETON STORIES

I enjoyed reading your book as it brought back
memories of Cape Breton, especially Glace Bay.
I could visualize everything you described.

You dip your pen in our unshed tears and tell stories
about women who do what is expected of them.
You take us down to the undercurrents where loss
and betrayals and secrets swirl around, where
some wounds scab over without healing.

To Ruth and Stan with Best Wishes. Jess

Remembrance
of Love
and other
Cape Breton
stories

Jess Bond

Jess Bond

express publications

Picton, Ontario, Canada

Remembrance of Love
and Other Cape Breton Stories
Copyright © 2004, Jess Bond

ISBN: 0-9735002-1-2
**For more information or
to order additional copies, please contact:**

Jess Bond
15 Wellington St. Apt. 204
Stirling, Ontario, Canada K0K 3E0
jess.bond@sympatico.ca

published by express publications
RR3 Picton, Ontario, Canada K0K 2T0
www.expresspublications.net
Printed in Canada by
Blitzprint Inc.

For Omar, Murray, Hazel and Marguerite

TABLE OF CONTENTS

GOD FORBID
THAT ANYTHING
SHOULD HAPPEN

O n a warm June Saturday morning, Cleo Murphy lingered over her morning tea. She loved Saturdays. When she was working, she used to put all her teaching preparation aside and give herself Saturday morning to read for pleasure. Now that she was retired she continued the habit. House and yard chores could wait. If only she had a handy husband like Archie, she would spend the whole day reading.

Cleo was sitting on her back verandah, watching the McKays who lived in the miner's house next door. Maybelle had him working on the porch screens. She was supervising and Archie was hammering. Retired from the pit a year ago, he now had another full-time job; carrying out Maybelle's endless orders.

Poor bugger, Cleo thought. She never gives him a minute's peace with all her demands. And she's so ungrateful. I wouldn't be ungrateful if he were my husband. Then she thought, the Bible says it's a sin to covet your neighbour's wife. It's likely it's also a sin to covet your neighbour's husband.

Cleo and Maybelle had grown up together, were in the same classroom all through grade school and high school. Cleo had been the serious one, the studious one, graduating with high marks and going off to Truro to get her teachers' license.

Maybelle had squeaked through the eleventh grade, got pregnant, and was married before the summer was over. Her white wedding gown was exquisite, and her wedding was one of the most lavish the town had ever seen. The town gossips had a great time going on about a big wedding being poor taste in wartime.

It was the third year of the war, sugar and butter rationed. The main topic of conversation at the wedding reception was where the hell did they get the ingredients for the wedding cake and all those rich squares.

No one, except family and Cleo knew that Maybelle was three months pregnant. Even if the guests had known that, the source of the baking ingredients would still have been the main topic of conversation.

Cleo was maid of honor. She wore a nauseous green gown of Maybelle's choosing. It made Cleo look as if she were suffering with a migraine. She remembered how quiet Archie was that day. He looked nervous and overwhelmed. His pale blonde hair, almost white, was slicked down, close to his scalp. His washed-out blue eyes avoided looking at Cleo when she tried to engage him in conversation.

Archie hadn't changed much over the years. Now his hair was really white, his eyes paler than ever, his long thin face still looking confused about the hand life had dealt him. Cleo often thought that if their baby had lived, or if they had had another baby or two, Archie's life would have been different.

Times when Cleo was alone with Archie, she itched to massage his shoulders to help him relax. They were seldom alone. On evenings Maybelle was doing her girls'-night-out thing, Cleo would call a few friends in for a game of cards and Archie would join them.

Cleo saw Archie in other social situations, but there was one evening a month she had him all to herself. Archie was a voracious reader.

He and Cleo passed books back and forth, then discussed them over the back fence. They quit talking about books in front of Maybelle after the day she snapped, "For Cripes sake, Cleo, I asked you over for a cup of tea, not so you and Archie could go on about those stupid books you read. If you two have to talk books, do it on your own time."

Cleo had formed a Book Club three years ago, the first year of her retirement. Archie wouldn't join because the members were all women. A day or so after the monthly book club meeting, Archie would let Cleo know that Maybelle was going out so he was free to spend the evening with her. It was like a secret date, even though Maybelle knew they were meeting to talk books.

In her teens, all Maybelle ever talked about was her appearance and how many boys were after her. While Cleo had her nose in Shakespeare or Dickens, Maybelle read movie magazines. She had a different hair style every week, fashioned after her two favourite movie stars, Betty Grable and Rita Hayworth. She would say to Cleo, "For God's sake, do something with your hair and wear some lipstick. You wouldn't be half bad looking if you'd pay some attention to your looks. God, if I see that old navy skirt and white blouse on you one more time, I'm going to throw up."

Cleo couldn't afford the kind of clothes that Maybelle wore. Maybelle's dad was a mine foreman. Cleo's dad was killed in the pit when she was ten years old. Her mother worked to support the family.

In her teens, Cleo was tall and skinny. She had dark brown curly hair, dark brown eyes. Her best feature was her smile. She didn't have any trouble attracting boys, and had no trouble finding herself a good man to marry when she was ready to get married.

Her last year in school was the last year of the war, and the single Bay Boys who survived the war were not only grateful to make it home alive, they were eager to marry and begin a family.

Cleo had twelve wonderful years with her Dave. He died suddenly with a heart attack when their daughter Sandra was nine years old. Sandra was Cleo's reason for picking up the pieces. She knew she had to make a life for her daughter and herself, and she did just that.

Here I am, comparing herself to Maybelle again. Cleo got up to make fresh tea when Maybelle arrived, holding out a plate of muffins.

"Pour me a cup of tea. I made your favourite muffins. Oatmeal and cranberries."

"How about Archie? He's the one working."

"If he stops now, he'll find something else to do. I want those screens finished this morning."

"Poor Archie."

"Poor Archie! Poor asshole! Those screens were supposed to be done a month ago. I swear to God that man deliberately puts things off to antagonize me." She spread butter on a muffin and waved it around as she recited her litany of complaints about Archie.

Cleo interrupted her. "I've heard that list many times, Maybelle."

"Yeah, well, you didn't hear this before. I still get the come-on from men, you know. God forbid that anything should happen to Archie, but I'm telling you, the next time I pick a husband, it will be a live one. Here's something else you haven't heard." She took a swig of tea. "Archie hasn't got any air left in his tire. We haven't had sex the past few years."

Cleo wanted to tell Maybelle she was sick of her talking about Archie behind his back, but she didn't want to deal with the fallout. She said, "I told you before, Maybelle, your sex life is an out-of-bounds topic." *As is my sex life. Are you remotely interested in how long it's been since I've had sex?*

A few weeks after that Saturday, Cleo was getting ready to visit Sandra and her family in Halifax. Cleo had been spending the first week of July in Halifax for several years. The end of the school year. Her two grandsons, eight and ten years old, full of energy had a dozen plans for their Nanny. Sandra and her husband, both teachers, wanting to do nothing but take some recovery time. That's where Cleo came in. She took the boys on outings. She loved having them to herself.

Archie arrived at the back door ready to drive her into the Sydney train station. When he was putting her bag in the trunk of the car, he told her, "Maybelle says she'd like to come to see you off but it's too early in the day for her to get up. She said to tell you to have a good trip and to say hello to Sandra for her." He gave her his shy grin. "Actually, I'm glad she isn't coming. I finished reading Somerset Maugham's book, *Then and Now*, and this will give us a chance to talk about it."

"Good, you know how much I love historical novels."

The half-hour trip to the railway station seemed to take only minutes. Archie stammered, "I'll miss you." as she boarded the train. She pretended not to hear him. "Thanks for driving me in, Archie. See you in a week."

A week later, Archie and Maybelle were waiting for her when she got off the train. Cleo laughed when Maybelle, instead of getting in the front seat with Archie, climbed into the back seat with her. Cleo leaned forward and touched Archie on the shoulder. "Should I say, "home James?" This is the first time I've ever had a chauffeur."

She could see Archie's eyes in the rear view mirror. He looked as if he were ready to chew nails.

Maybelle spoke. "Are you surprised that I'm here to meet your train?" She didn't pause long enough for an answer. "I can't wait to tell you something." She gave Cleo a little shove. "Reg McDonald has come back to Cape Breton to live!" Her face was flushed with excitement. "Imagine! You knew that his wife died a few years ago. His mother had left him that lovely old house on South Street, which Reg has been renting out. Well, he wrote to tell the tenants he would be moving home in a few weeks."

Then she dug an elbow into Cleo's side. "Remember the crush you two had on each other in high school?"

"For God's sake, Maybelle! Reg and I are almost sixty years old. I've run into him the summers he came home from Toronto for a visit, and I have to tell you, I think he's turned into a very boring man."

"Well, I think it'll be exciting having a new man around."

"So will every widow in town, not to mention the gals who never married. They'll be standing in line."

Maybelle gave her a hard shove. "I just knew you'd make light of this. You're never going to have a better chance to get a man."

"God, don't start that again. How many times have I told you I like my life just the way it is."

"Well, for sure, you're too set in your ways for marriage. I'm talking about having some fun. Having a man to take you places, maybe even go on a trip somewhere." She wagged a finger in Cleo's face. After all, Cleo, we've been friends all our lives. I guess I should know what you need."

I wish I knew what I needed, Cleo thought. *What would you say, Maybelle if I told you that there are days when I think it would be kind of nice to have good old Archie taking care of me the way he takes care of you?*

Archie was grumbling to himself in the front seat.

"Change the subject, Maybelle. I know you mean well, but I'm telling you that if you think you're going to begin a match-making project, you can just forget it."

Maybelle turned away from her and stared out the window. "Suit yourself. I was only trying to be a good friend."

"Well, good friends know how to mind their own business." She was sorry the minute the words were out of her mouth. She knew she had hurt Maybelle's feelings. Despite their differences, she and Maybelle were friends. Lifelong friends. Cleo had several teacher friends she felt closer to, but Maybelle was more like a sister.

That evening, after she had unpacked her things and made herself a bite of supper, Cleo decided to go for a walk along the cliff. Five minutes from her house she could see the cliff was deserted. The evening was cool. The salt wind blowing up from the ocean cleared her head, and the sound of the waves hitting the shore were a comfort to her. Her solitary walks along the cliff were part of her survival all those years ago. She walked for thirty minutes, then turned and headed home.

Archie was sitting on his front verandah alone having his evening cigar. Maybelle never joined him because she hated his cigars. Cleo thought Archie didn't look like a cigar man, but the evenings he came to her place to play cards, she would suggest he have one. She loved the relaxed look on his face as he puffed away.

"Maybelle told me to ask you in for a snack. I think she's upset about having words with you in the car."

"Tell her thanks, Archie, but I'm tired from the day. Tell her we'll have tea together in the morning." She turned and went toward her house, not giving him a chance to say anything else.

When Dave died, it took every ounce of energy in her body to put one foot in front of the other, to find ways to help Sandra bear the loss of the daddy she loved so much.

She could never forget how Maybelle and Archie did everything possible to help her through the bad patches.

When Dave died, Cleo didn't want to get stuck in the grieving widow role. She knew keeping busy was important and she thanked God for her work. She concentrated on the happy memories he left behind. She was grateful for the good life they had shared and she was determined to do her best to honor those happy memories.

She and Dave used to begin and end their days with talk. They both loved to talk. Over breakfast it was planning talk. Planning the day, planning the weekend, planning the cottage they would build on the Mira River someday.

At night, snug in bed, they talked love talk. He would say something like, "I've thought of two more reasons why I love you."

She would say something like, "Tell me one of the secrets in your heart."

The night of her return from Halifax , her last thought as she dropped off to sleep was, *I guess I just haven't met another man I could look in the eye and say, "Tell me one of the secrets in your heart."*

Three weeks later, she was having her first date with Reg MacDonald. He called and asked if he could take her out to dinner. Before she could respond, he added, "I've made reservations for the dining room at the Atlantic Hotel in Sydney. They serve the best steaks on the island."

Cleo was putting the kettle on for tea the next morning when Maybelle, still in her housecoat, arrived. "Come on, girl, tell me the details!"

"People usually knock before entering somebody's kitchen. What if Reg had spent the night and we were standing here in our birthday suits?

Maybelle snorted. "Fat chance of that. I watched him walking you to your front door at ten." She waved her hands. "Don't just stand there. Get that tea made. I hope you have some whole wheat bread for toast."

When Cleo said nothing, Maybelle muttered, "For cripes sake, Cleo, can't you make toast and talk at the same time?"

Ten minutes later when Cleo finished describing the dinner, the people they knew who were also having dinner at the Atlantic, and Reg's plans for the house on South Street, Maybelle said, "Doesn't sound like a very exciting evening to me. Didn't you talk about anything personal?"

"It was a pleasant evening. Period." She wasn't about to tell Reg's talk of how unhappy his marriage had been, how there would have been a divorce if they hadn't been Catholic. She sure wasn't going to tell Maybelle that he had someone special in his life and that he had asked her to move to Cape Breton with him. Maybelle could find that out for herself. When Reg had said to her, "You're a swell person, Cleo. I'm hoping you'll be friends with Sara," Cleo knew why he had asked her out. He wanted her to be the Welcome Lady.

"The important thing is, did he ask you out again?" Maybelle asked.

Cleo nodded. *And I surprised myself by accepting, even though I have the feeling it will be as boring as it was last evening.* She slapped a plate of toast in front of Maybelle. "Can we change the subject?"

Maybelle slathered marmalade on her toast. "Tell me what he was wearing. How much has he changed?"

Cleo sighed and joined Maybelle at the table. "You're not going to let up, are you?" She took a sip if her tea. "Well, he was wearing a dark grey tailored suit and white shirt, blue speckled tie. Remember the thick head of black hair he had when he was young? Well, he still has it, except it's white, and as it was when he was young, every hair is in place. He's still handsome, still conceited. Oh yes, I forgot. He has a paunch."

"What about plans for the second date?"

"I invited him here for a game of cards. Told him it would give him a chance to see some old friends. I'm planning on two tables. He's also interested in joining our Book Club."

Maybelle emptied her tea into the sink. She slammed her tea cup on the counter and headed for the door. "Cleo. There are times I could just shake the livin' daylights out of you. I just don't understand you."

"That's O.K. kiddo. There are times I don't understand myself."

She followed Maybelle to the door. "Are you coming to my card party? It's this coming Saturday night."

Maybelle's voice was full of sarcasm." I wouldn't miss it for the world."

"Will you make your famous pineapple squares?"

Maybelle stomped out without answering.

The card party was a disaster. Maybelle made an ass of herself. She arrived late when everyone was sitting at the card tables, sipping drinks, chatting and waiting for the game to begin. She was decked out in a pale blue chiffon dress, a dress meant for a garden party, not a card party. Her hair was blonder than usual and she was wearing her best jewelry." The other women, including Cleo, were wearing summer slacks and casual tops.

One of the women said to Cleo, "You didn't tell us this was dress-up," then turned to Maybelle. "Honey, Archie's been here for over an hour. Looks like it took you that long to rig yourself out."

Maybelle ignored her. She held out a plate. "Hope everyone likes pineapple squares." She walked over to the sideboard and added them to the array of sweets and sandwiches on display. Cleo said to her, "For God's sake sit down, and let's get on with the card game."

Maybelle pouted. "I didn't hurry because I knew Reg would have a lot of catching up to do with his old friends." She stared at Reg as if she could eat him with a spoon. Archie's face turned red with embarrassment.

Cleo thought the whole evening was like a scene from a drawing room farce. No one was paying much attention to the card game.

At nine o'clock, Cleo went out to the kitchen to put the kettle on for tea. Archie followed her. He muttered, "That woman can't let five minutes go by without talking about herself."

"Never mind, Archie. The game is almost over. Here, help me pass the tea cups around."

At ten o'clock Reg said it was time he was on his way.

Maybelle leaned across the table and said, "But Reg, you haven't begun to tell us your plans for the house renovations."

One of the women stood up. "He can save that for another time, Maybelle. I've got a busy day tomorrow."

Cleo refused Maybelle's offer to wash up. "Let's leave

it until tomorrow morning."

She waited until she was sure everyone was out of sight of the house before she poured herself a glass of white wine and moved out on the back verandah. It was dark as midnight outside. Cleo's pots of artificial pink geraniums on her kitchen windows were the only bit of color visible.

She wished for a breeze. She took a sip of wine. *I'm glad they're all gone and I have my veranda to myself.* She experienced profound relief that the evening was over. Cleo decided there wasn't going to be a next time. At that moment she looked up to see Archie making his way across the yard to join her.

When he sat down, Cleo asked, "Is Maybelle coming over? Shall I get two more glasses?"

He shook his head. "She's in bed watching a movie. I came over because there's something I have to ask you."

Cleo waited.

"Are you interested in Reg McDonald?"

"No, Archie. I'm not interested in Reg MacDonald. And Reg MacDonald is not interested in me."

"Thank God." Archie rarely said more than a sentence or two at a time, but at that moment he launched into what was, for him, a speech. "Cleo, you know me. You know I believe in the sanctity of marriage, and that I would never leave Maybelle." He stopped for a second. "God forbid that anything should happen to Maybelle, but I've got to know, Cleo. If anything should happen to her, would you consider marrying me?" He held out his hands to her, then dropped them, then held them out again, his palms turned up in a gesture of futility.

Poor, dear old Archie, Cleo thought. She said, "No,

Archie. I plan never to re-marry. She reached out and touched him. "But if I did re-marry, it would be to a man like you."

He stood up. "Thanks for saying that, Cleo."

When he was gone, the tears came. The only person she wanted to tell about Archie's proposal was Dave. She hadn't missed him so acutely for a long time. She remembered how his arms felt when he reached out for her, how intently he listened to her when she told him things. She decided to have a good cry. Sometimes there was nothing else to do but have a good cry.

FRANNY'S GIRL

ive a.m. Franny lay in the spoon position against her husband's back. She moved away from Richard carefully. He was a light sleeper and she didn't want to wake him. She knew she wouldn't be able to get back to sleep, and she knew that it was thinking about the little girl she had seen that morning that was causing her wide- awake state.

What Franny actually saw was the reflection of the girl, her big eyes staring at a dress in the Metropolitan window. The look of intense yearning on the child's face made Franny want to rush into the store and buy the dress for her, but she couldn't. She was in a hurry to get home to make Richard's lunch.

Franny knew all about wanting something you couldn't have. There was something about the back of the child's skinny legs and the look of sadness on her thin little face that filled Franny's head with memories of her own childhood. With all her heart Franny wished that the little girl was lucky enough to have the kind of grandmother that she had had.

The best thing that ever happened in Franny's life was that her parents - her young, irresponsible parents - before heading for Toronto to look for work - parked her with Grandma. Franny was six at the time and until then, saw little of her grandmother. Weekends were the only time. Wonderful weekends. Grandma's good cooking. Getting to wear the pretty dresses Grandma made for her to wear to church. Being tucked into bed with a bedtime story.

Grandma had a thing about liquor. She wouldn't let her daughter and husband into her house if they smelled of beer, which was most of the time, and she wouldn't visit them because of the way they lived, their house uncared for, one drinking party after another. But she did come to get her often for visits.

One time she recalled, Grandma had come to the door about seven Saturday morning to pick her up. As usual, she knocked at the door until Franny answered it. Everyone else in the house was sleeping off the party of the night before.

When Franny put a finger to her lips and then whispered, "They're all asleep Grandma," her grandmother whispered back, "A thunder and lightening storm wouldn't disturb that lot." Then she shook her head. "They've a strange way to celebrate the end of the war. The damn war's been over for three months."

Franny remembered the last weekend she had seen her parents. They took her to her grandmother, her few clothes in a paper bag, and announced their plans to drive to Toronto. Her father claimed he had enough of living dangerously in Sicily. He wasn't going to work in the pit anymore. He was off to Toronto to find a safe job.

Franny's mother passed their house key to Grandma. "Ma, hold onto this for me. We might have to come back if we don't find work. If we do find work, sell our few sticks of furniture and send us the money." That was it. Not even a kiss good-bye. A wave of the hand and they were gone.

They were hit head-on by a truck on Highway 2 just outside of Kingston. The driver of the truck survived but Franny's parents were killed instantly.

Before Grandma turned over the house key to the coal company, she and Franny gathered up a few things from the house and left the rest for the new tenants.

Thus began Franny's new life. A safe and predictable life. She woke up every morning in a clean bed, put on washed and ironed clothes, had cereal for breakfast, said morning prayers with Grandma, and then the two of them would plan the day.

Life with Grandma didn't have any leftover nickels after the groceries and heat and lights were paid for. Grandma had a small pension from the coal company and free rent in their company house. Franny's grandfather had died before she was born. Grandma could stretch a dollar like no one else. She owned a Sunday dress and a Sunday coat and hat. Her other clothes, always clean and pressed, she had forever. Franny's clothes were hand-me-downs from a cousin, her spoiled cousin Janice, who had every new fad that came along. Franny, was more than glad to get Janice's pretty things.

One day, when she came home from school crying because some girls in her class were taunting her because she had to wear her cousins cast-offs, Grandma rolled her eyes and said, "Franny those girls are jealous. Why the beautiful dresses and skirts and sweaters Janice passes on to you are fit for a princess. Now you invite those girls home one day. I'll make my famous lemon loaf and my famous fat molasses cookies. They'll have something else to be jealous about."

Franny liked it when Grandma spoke to her as if she were another grown-up. She was always explaining things to her like how to read the maps in the old atlas that had belonged to Grandfather, why some people acted the way they did, why school was the most important thing in her young life.

Evenings, when Franny's homework was finished, they played cards or read. Sometimes Grandma managed to save some brown sugar and cocoa to make a batch of chocolate fudge. If one of Grandma's friends dropped in, Grandma always asked Franny to read a story to the ladies.

Franny thought she was the luckiest girl in the world. She knew that she did well in life, and in her nursing career because of the kind of childhood Grandma had fashioned for her.

Franny stretched her legs, being careful not to disturb Richard. She began thinking about blueberry season. Warm July days, perfect for berry picking. Franny was going to miss her boys. She depended on them to help her pick enough blueberries to preserve so there would be blueberry pies come winter. Richard made himself scarce on picking days, but she noticed that he ate more than his share of pies and blueberry muffins and blueberry pudding.

Their twins, Tommy and Michael, had just completed first year university and were off on a summer job planting evergreens on the north end of the Island.

The day they set out, Tommy teased his dad. "Dad, you're gonna have to go blueberry picking with her, like it or not."

Richard snapped his newspaper at him. "Is that so?"

Not bloody likely he'll offer to come picking berries with me, Franny thought.

As if reading her mind, Richard said, "Sweetheart, you must have a couple of friends who would love to go picking berries with you."

She didn't answer. She concentrated on Dear Abby, pretending she didn't hear him. Franny knew the first hour was Richard's favourite time of the day. The two of them finishing off the breakfast coffee, reading the morning paper, sometimes reading parts of the paper to each other, sometimes having heated discussions about this or that, sometimes Franny would reach for her memo pad and remind Richard of errands that had to be done.

Come nine o'clock, Franny would look around their big, comfortable kitchen, and say. "Time to plan the day, Richard."

For her it was kitchen tidy-up, shower, dress, make the bed, back to the kitchen and her memo pad. She planned lunch and supper, then listed the chores and any meetings she had to attend. She volunteered several hours a week in the town library and the seniors' home.

For Richard, it was a leisurely shower, getting dressed and heading for town and his Clock and Watch Shop. He not only sold beautiful clocks and watches, but repaired them as well. Franny often teased Richard about living with clocks, and being totally incapable of ever being on time.

That evening, when Franny and Richard were having their before-bed cup of tea, Franny said, "If I had a daughter, she could come berry picking with me."

Richard groaned, "Oh God, are you going to start on that again?"

"The house is awfully empty with the boys living in Halifax." She gave him her most beguiling smile. "We don't have to adopt a little girl, Richard. Since we're in our forties, I doubt that we could, but we could be foster parents to her."

He slammed his cup on the saucer. "Franny, as much as I love our boys, you know I've been looking forward to having the place to ourselves." He started to tick off on his fingers, "No tripping over sports equipment, no having that damn rock music roaring up the stairs from the rec room, no having countless pairs of feet pounding down the same stairs day and night."

"There wouldn't be those things with a little girl." When tears began to roll down her face, he held up his hands as if to ward her off. "Darlin', please. No tears. Please Franny. There's been very little I've denied you. You know that."

She nodded and gave him a sad little smile. "I know, Richard. I know."

That day, as Franny went about her house chores, her thoughts turned to ways of winning Richard over. When the doctor told her, after the birth of the twins, that she wouldn't be able to have more children, she cried her heart out. The doctor had scolded her, told her to be grateful that she had two healthy sons. She was grateful, but the wish for a daughter had never gone away.

When the boys began school she began her campaign to adopt a girl. At that time she was dreaming of a newborn baby girl. Richard said, "That isn't an option for us, Franny. We've got our hands full raising the twins." His voice was emphatic and his face wore a final expression.

It seemed she just turned around and the boys were in high school. They were sons to be proud of, doing well in school, involved in volunteer activities, never a dull moment with their antics. She still longed for a daughter.

The way Franny finally got her wish had to do with one of Richard's watches.

A week after Franny had broached the subject of taking in a foster child, they were sitting at the kitchen table, drinking coffee and reading the morning paper.

Richard put down his paper. "I forgot to tell you something that happened at the shop yesterday."

Franny refilled their coffee mugs. "What's that?"

"I caught a girl stealing a watch. An expensive watch." He shook his head. "She looked to be about ten. A skinny little thing. I thought it strange for her not to be in school. I was just about to go to talk to her, when I saw her reach for the watch and slip it into her sweater coat pocket, box and all."

"Oh, my God,Richard, what did you do?"

"The first thing I did was retrieve the watch and put it back on the display shelf. Then the wailing started. I couldn't get her to stop long enough to talk to me. Finally, I told her if she didn't stop bawling I was going to call the police. She grabbed my hands." "Please mister, don't." Then she gave me the most pathetic, pleading look. "It's my mother's birthday and I don't have any money to buy her a present."

I told her I couldn't let her walk out of the shop without talking to one of her parents. I asked her for her phone number. More bawling. When she found out I wasn't giving in, she gave me a number."

"What did the poor little thing look like Richard?"

Franny's heart turned over when Richard said, "She looked like a pixie. Pointed little chin and huge green eyes. Straight black hair. Skinny as a bean pole, but she did have a charming smile. I gave her a chocolate bar to eat while we waited for her mother. She was a gabby little thing. Talked a blue streak about hating school. Turns out the kid doesn't have a mother. She's living in that group foster home on Sydney Street, and the woman who came for her was one of the workers at the home. The young woman, a Miss Biggs, thanked me for calling, then turned a worried face to the kid. "Amy, you're lucky this nice man called us and not the police." Then she turned to me and said quietly, "This is the third time this month she's been caught shoplifting." Then she heaved a sigh, thanked me and left, holding the kid by the hand."

When he told her that, Franny's eyes filled with tears. "I'm sure she was the child I saw downtown yesterday. There's got to be a reason she's stealing, Richard. You know the saying, "Rather be wanted for murder than not wanted at all."

Richard shook his head. "I suppose you want to rush right down to that foster place and move her in here, bag and baggage." He stared at Franny in disbelief. "Jesus, Franny, the kid's a thief!."

"She's a little girl who needs help. Richard."

"I agree the kid needs help, Franny. And guess what? We're not getting involved."

Franny's thoughts tumbled around a mile a minute. There had to be some way she could change Richard's mind.

The next day, a Friday, was the day Franny gave a few hours to the seniors' home, also the day she picked up Richard at the shop. They had a standing date for lunch at Lowrey's Family Restaurant.

When she walked into the clock shop, Richard was standing, hands on his hips, scowling down at a little girl. "Are you looking for a gift for your mother again?"

The girl of the long black hair and pixie face, flashed him a sweet smile. "I asked Miss Biggs if I could come, Mister. I came to thank you for not calling the police yesterday."

Franny spoke, "You must be Amy. What a nice thing for you to do." When Amy turned and looked up at Franny the sadness in her big green eyes melted Franny's heart.

"How do you know my name? Who are you?"

"I'm Mister's wife, and I came by to take him out for lunch." Impulsively, she added, "Would you like to come with us?"

Before Richard could say a word, Franny said, "I'm going to call Miss Biggs and tell her we're taking you out to lunch, and that we'll take you home afterwards."

Leah Lowrey always waited on their table on Fridays, making a great fuss when serving them. When she walked toward them, her pad in hand, Franny said, "We have a new friend with us today, Leah. This is Amy."

Leah rolled her eyes. "I know Amy. She's been here before."

Richard cleared his throat, but said nothing. When their food arrived, he concentrated on eating his fish and chips as Franny and Amy gabbed away.

The green eyes stared into Franny's face. "You're the nicest woman I ever met in my whole life. You look like my mother."

"Amy, do you mind my asking where your mother lives?"

"She's dead. She died of a broken heart."

Richard thought, *I wonder where she planned to mail the watch she was stealing*, but he said nothing.

"What about your father, dear?"

"He was killed in the pit when I was five."

Richard cleared his throat again. "Amy, you better finish up your fish and chips. We don't want Miss Biggs worried about you."

She gave him another heart-breaker smile. "Thank you for taking me to lunch, Mister. Nobody's ever taken me out to lunch before."

When they delivered Amy, Franny told Richard she was going to walk home.

He said, "You're pissed off at me, aren't you? Well, if anyone should be pissed off it's me."

"I've seen you treat strangers better than you treated that poor, sweet, little girl," Franny scolded.

Richard got into the car and slammed the door. Franny turned heel and walked up the street. She didn't plan to go home. As soon as Richard's car was out of sight, she was going to have a talk with Miss Biggs at the foster home.

Miss Biggs told her things she'd rather not have known about Amy. It was true that the child's father had been killed in the pit, but Amy lied about her mother being dead. According to records, the mother had headed for Toronto with another man when Amy was only three years old. Amy had been five when her father was killed.

When Franny asked if Amy had been in foster homes, Miss Biggs closed her eyes and nodded her head. "Five so far."

Franny waited expectantly for more information, but Miss Biggs sat there staring out the window of her office. Finally, she said. "There is something endearing about Amy. She can be very sweet in many ways, but we just can't stop her from stealing and lying. She's good at both, and when she's found out, she has these long, complicated reasons. More lies of course."

"Has she had psychological help?"

"Of course, and she's managed to manipulate more than one of the counselors. Especially men counselors. Men seem to be putty in Amy's hands."

When Franny said, "I know we could give her a good home. I'd spend a lot of time with her, and she could never put anything over on my husband, Richard. He's strict, but very loving and fair." Miss Biggs looked horrified. She held both her hands in front of her face and waved them from side to side. "You have no idea what you are contemplating. Amy is more than a handful. I haven't begun to tell you some of her problems."

"How about a trial period of a month? Surely that would

be enough time to see if Richard and I would make suitable foster parents."

Miss Biggs's face took on a new expression. No words, but the look said, *a whole month without Amy.*

Franny took the long way home. She was planning how to get Richard to agree to keeping Amy for a trial period.

That evening, Franny served Richard his favourite pot roast dinner, along with a bottle of his favourite wine. When Franny served the coffee and apple pie, Richard picked up his fork and waved it at her. "Out with it. I know this is about the kid."

"I spoke to Miss Biggs this afternoon," she began.

He stirred cream into his coffee, saying nothing.

"Miss Briggs thinks we might be able to take Amy for a trial period of a month." When he remained silent, she burst out, "For God's sake, Richard, say something!"

Richard folded his arms and sat back in his chair. "You don't want to hear what I really want to say." Then he reached across the table for one of her hands. "Dearest Franny, I think that kid means trouble, but I could sit here and talk 'til the cows come home and you wouldn't have heard a word I said."

When he said, "You might as well find out for yourself," Franny jumped up from the table, ran to him and showered his face with kisses.

His voice was stern. "We're going to sit the kid down and make it clear that she's here for a month only. And she's to call us by our first names. We're not to be called mommy and daddy. We'll tell her we're giving her a bit of a summer holiday. We can do that for her. Take her to the beach. I wouldn't mind a couple of days fishing in the Bras' Dor lakes. We can drive out to Mira for picnics. I mean it, Franny. I don't want the kid to get the idea that she's going to be living here forever."

Franny threw back her head and laughed. "Darling, you forgot to mention berry picking."

Amy had been with them a few days before Richard spoke about the kissing. It was Amy's bedtime, and fresh from her bath, she came into the living room to say good-night before she went upstairs for the bedtime read. When she threw herself at Richard and wound her skinny arms around his neck, he put a finger against her mouth. "No more kissing me on the mouth, Amy." The kissing he referred to was not a peck, but a long, sloppy, smacky kiss.

"But that's they way they kiss on T.V."

Franny said, "That's right, dear. But this isn't T.V. Richard and I will settle for kisses on the cheek."

Amy gave them a goofy smile. "O.K., whatever you say."

The rest of the week passed smoothly. Franny observed Amy watching them and imitating them, going out of her way to please. She wanted to say to Richard, "See, how she's responding to being in a loving home, being taken care of?" She decided to wait. It was just as well she did.

A shopping trip was planned for Saturday morning. Franny had already bought Amy two new sundresses and two pair of shorts and two T-shirts. She couldn't wait to do a major shopping for her.

It was a perfect July morning as the two of them set out for town, each carrying a large shopping bag. Amy's dark eyes sparkled with excitement and Franny's happiness was all over her face.

That evening, supper eaten and dishes cleared away, the fashion show was on. Franny told Richard to settle in his favourite chair in the living room. "I'll pour you another mug of coffee."

They both laughed as Amy paraded up and down the livingroom, hands on hips, doing a model swagger. Franny had told Amy to save her new jeans and jean jacket for the last, and when she minced around the living room in the jean outfit, Franny went into Amy's bedroom to hang up the new clothes.

When she was putting things on hangers, she saw the bulge under one of the pillows. She found two cotton print halters and a red bathing suit, price tags still on them, halters and bathing suit that Franny hadn't bought. Her heart felt squeezed. She would have to tell Richard. She didn't want to tell Richard, but she would have to tell him. She would talk to Amy first.

Later, the bedtime story read, Amy held up her arms for a good-night hug. "This was the very best day I ever had, Franny."

"Something spoiled today for me, Amy." When Amy stared at her, Franny reached under the pillow for the halters and bathing suit.

Amy sat up in bed. "I was going to tell you tomorrow. Honest, Franny."

"Did you steal these things, Amy?"

"Gosh, no! Miss Biggs gave me some money. I didn't tell you about the halters and bathing suit because you were buying me so many things and I didn't want you to think I was a greedy-guts. But, honest, Franny, I was going to tell you tomorrow."

"Do you have the sales slip?"

"I didn't wait for one."

Franny tucked Amy in. She would call Miss Biggs to check on whether or not she had given Amy money. She said, "We'll talk more about this tomorrow, Amy."

When she joined Richard in the living room, he asked her, "What's up? You look like you lost a friend."

She told him about the halter and bathing suit. He didn't say, "I told you so." He didn't say, "I'm not surprised." He put his arms around her and held her close. "Amy and I will go to town on Monday and she will return the things. Don't let this one incident spoil your time with Amy, Sweetheart."

Before going to bed that night, Franny and Richard looked in on Amy. She was curled up, sound asleep, one thumb in her mouth.

"She looks like a sweet little angel, doesn't she?" Franny whispered.

"She looks like a troubled little bugger to me," Richard whispered back.

The incidents of stealing and telling lies escalated in the third week.

One of Franny's bracelets had gone missing. A twenty-dollar bill disappeared from Richard's wallet. It was Richard's decision that they wouldn't confront Amy about the missing items. They were at the kitchen table, having a second coffee. He said, "There's only a week and a half left of her visit. Let's be careful about leaving things around to tempt her."

When he said that, Franny shook her head. "I just don't understand. She's been so good, Richard, so polite and appreciative. She loves the morning play group, and she's so full of happy stories when she comes home for lunch."

That was the day they had a call from one of the teachers of the play program, telling them that Amy had begun to leave the church playground an hour earlier than closing time.

When Amy arrived home from lunch that day, she was accompanied by a young policeman, Matt King. Matt was the son of a friend of Richard's.

Franny passed Amy a sandwich and glass of milk. "Amy, sit out on the deck and eat this while we talk."

Amy squinted her eyes at the three of them. "Sure, you're gonna believe him. Aren'tcha? You won't listen to my side. Nobody ever wants to hear my side."

Franny took Amy's shoulder bag from her. "Please, Franny. The stuff in there is mine. My mother sent me some money. Honest." Matt interrupted. "When I was called to the store, I paid for those things, Amy, and you know it. I did that because Franny and Richard are friends of mine.

Franny settled Amy on the deck and then joined the men in the kitchen. Matt was saying, "She's been hanging around with a rough bunch at the shopping centre. My advice is to you is take Amy back to the group home. That kid is like a loose cannon. You don't have the resources to handle her. She needs the close supervision the home workers supply."

Richard shook his head. "We promised the kid a month with us. We'll keep that promise." He reached for one of Franny's hands. "I'll close the shop for a week and we'll take her on a real holiday." Then he turned to Matt. "We know enough about kids to know that Amy is hurting."

Matt gave a large sigh. "That's one way to put it. She was sexually abused in her last foster home. First, the bastard won her over, treated her like a princess before the abuse began. His wife, who wasn't keen on taking in a foster child, blew the whistle on him. It was a strange situation. Amy wouldn't testify against him. Said he loved her and she loved him."

Franny covered her ears. "Oh God, don't tell us anymore."

When Matt left, Richard and Franny joined Amy on the deck.

"You're gonna send me back to Miss Biggs, aren'tcha?"

Richard said, "Amy, we promised you a month with us, and we're going to keep our promise. Franny and I know that life has been tough for you. We know you have problems. When you go back to Miss Biggs, we're going to get you the kind of help you need. We'll still be your friends, and you can come visit us sometimes."

Amy shrugged her shoulder, said, "Sure, sure." Then her face crumpled. She started to bawl. "The first day I was here I knew you would never keep me. I knew it was too good to be true." She gave them each a defiant look. "I'm going upstairs. See ya at supper time."

Franny said quietly,"I thought if I loved her unconditionally, I could win her over. I truly believed that."

"I know you did, but you know as well as I do that sometimes love isn't enough. Maybe if we were younger. Maybe if Amy were only two or three years old." He held out his arms to her.

She stood quietly, her head on his shoulder. "Dear, it's time for me to give up my obsession about having a daughter."

"My God, don't say that Franny. The happy look on your face those first two weeks Amy was with us was wondrous to see. It made me realize how important that dream was to you. Don't give up. And we won't lose touch with Amy."

"Amy and I didn't go berry picking yet." Franny's voice was expressionless.

"Well, for cripes sake, dig out the buckets. I hear McLeod's Crossing is loaded with blueberries this month. Tell Amy to put on her new jeans and jean jacket and get down here. The three of us are going berry picking this very afternoon."

A LITTLE FOOLISHNESS

Jane gave up asking to manage the household finances shortly after she and Joseph were married forty years ago. That she had worked as a bookkeeper didn't matter. Her husband's life-long obsession with saving was something she had learned to tolerate. Joseph's credo was he earned the money and he controlled how it was to be spent. Now he was dying.

If he lived one more month they would celebrate their fortieth anniversary. *Celebrate is a strange word to come to mind as I think of my marriage to Joseph. Will I celebrate my freedom from living with such a driven man for forty years? What will my days be like when I no longer have to cater to keep the peace? Will I like having my life back?*

The cancer was discovered when he recently had his yearly medical. The doctor asked her if she thought Joseph would want to know the truth. *The truth.* She had turned away from the question. *There's been little truth between Joseph and me. I don't believe it possible to deal with truth after years of the absence of truth.* She said to the doctor, "I'll leave that up to you."

On her daily visits to the hospital, Jane listened to Joseph's complaints, wrote down the instructions for things she was to do. She didn't try to understand what was going on in his head. She had stopped doing that a long time ago. Jane had spent forty years of her life with a man she never understood, and now he was dying. The first year they were married, she was shocked when she realized the length Joseph would go to to save a nickel. Jane understood his fear of poverty. His father's hardware business in the Steele Plant city where they lived went under during the depression. Joseph used to say repeatedly that his children were never going to have the childhood he experienced.

She understood his being a workaholic, but she never came to terms with his niggardliness.

Now she was observing Joseph's discomfort at having to talk about money and his business with her. Yesterday, at the moment of her leave-taking, he reminded her to see to it that their oldest son, Harry, would come to the hospital to see him that evening.

"Harry is swamped," she told him, "having to run the business without you. Why can't it wait until tomorrow? He's putting in pretty long days."

"Woman, I'm telling you to get him here. This evening." He half sat up, then fell back, gritting his teeth. "I had my lawyer here again this morning. Harry needs to sign some papers." Then he turned away from her. He let out a weak little grunt. "Just do it, Jane. Why is it so hard for you to do as I ask?"

She hadn't been able to reach Harry. His secretary told her that he was in Baddeck supervising the renovation of a hotel. It would have been easy to track Harry down, but she chose not to do so.

While she was thinking this, she was standing at her kitchen counter, lining the cake tin she used for her chocolate cake. Her best friend, Sarah, who was newly widowed, was coming to supper that evening.

Jane had been serving her special chocolate cake to friends with afternoon tea for years. It was a dark, moist cake, topped with a fluffy, fudge icing. Jane never cut into its sweetness that she didn't think of her mother. It was the recipe her mother used for the cake she served with afternoon tea. Her mother had been free to have friends in whenever she felt like it. Jane had to take a stand when Joseph told her he didn't want her feeding the neighbours chocolate cake.

As Jane scraped the rich batter into the pan, she thought about the awful fight she and Joseph had about the chocolate cake all those years ago. They had been sitting at the kitchen table, Joseph checking off the weekly grocery list written on the back of a used envelope.

She leaned across the table as he crossed out one of the items. "Why did you do that? Harry loves his cup of cocoa at bedtime, and I like to make my chocolate cake."

He didn't bother looking up. He just kept checking the list.

At first she tried coaxing. "Joseph, you know very well that I've pared spending to the bone. The few extra things are for a bit of baking."

"We can do without the baking."

The finality in his voice set her off. "Joseph, I help you save in every way I can. Sewing my own clothes. Sewing and knitting for Harry. Doing without." She knew her voice was full of bitterness. "Always doing without."

She remembered how difficult it had been not to cry. "Doing without," she said the words again. "And for what? So you can save another nickel. So you can squirrel money away. I might feel differently if I were a real partner in all this saving, but I don't even know how much money you make, or how much money you've saved."

Then she issued an ultimatum. "Either put the cocoa back on the list or you can get your own meals from now on." She got up carefully from the table. She was in her last month of pregnancy with their second son at the time. "I mean it Joseph. Put the cocoa back on the list or be prepared to get your own meals."

He grabbed the list and slammed out of the house. The cocoa was in the box of groceries he brought home that day. She knew it would be. He hated to cook. He didn't even like to make himself a cup of tea. But he loved to eat.

Strange that when we were young, our intimate life was so very different from the life we shared outside of the bedroom. We had both been greedy for sex. I remember how his handsome face softened when we made love, how he would say "Jane, Jane, Jane," over and over again when he climaxed.

When it was clear to her that the rules of penny-pinch-ing were engraved in stone, and were not going to change, she slowly fell out of love. She made the decision not to withhold sex because of the changes in her feelings toward him. She never used sex in exchange for anything. If he asked for it he got it.

After her second son's birth, when she knew she was completely out of love with Joseph, she began to make some changes in her life. She kept her new interests to herself, just as she hugged her secret thoughts and yearnings to herself.

She never once thought about getting out of the marriage. That wasn't an option. It was the forties, and divorce was rare. Just as rare as working mothers. Sure, women took over men's jobs during the war, but now that the war was over, many women returned home from the factories and offices. Men were back from the war, and they got job priority.

Harry was three, and Joey a baby when she began her search for new interests. She knew that if she wanted to find some enjoyment in life beside taking care of her boys, she would have to do it for herself.

The town library was her main source. At first, she brought home fiction, escape fiction. She loved historical novels. Then she began to read biographies. There was a lot to be learned from the lives of others. She also brought home lots of children's books to read aloud to the boys. Joseph acted annoyed if she read in the evenings, so she read in the afternoons when he was at work.

At the end of the war, Joseph began to buy up old houses and renovate them for sale or rent. He became so busy that he began to work from dawn until bedtime. She was free to read whenever she had the time.

She turned Sarah onto reading. When Sarah's husband, who was almost as controlling as Joseph, made nasty cracks about Sarah's library books, Sarah decided to keep her library books out of sight. Jane and Sarah had wonderful discussions about the books they read. They gave their get togethers a name-*The Secret Reading Club*. Those afternoons together got them through teething, measles, school problems, and the vagaries of living with difficult husbands.

Jane taught herself to sew and knit. She became an accomplished knitter, getting around the cost of wool by explaining to Joseph how much she could save by knitting the boys sweaters, socks, caps, and mittens.

A book on nutrition opened another world to her.

She learned how to make yogurt, how to increase the nutrition in the meals she served her family by adding wheat germ, bran, various seeds to her stews and soups, biscuits and bread. The Adele Davis book, *Eat Right to Keep Fit*, became her bible.

In berry season she picked blueberries and cranberries by the bucket and preserved them. She learned how to garden organically, and every September she canned and preserved for days on end.

She told Sarah one time, "The positive thing that has come out of having a husband who treats every dime as if it were the size of a manhole cover, is that it's forced me to become resourceful. I've learned so much about gardening and nutrition."

Sarah laughed at her. "How about making your own cold cream, shampoo, cleaning products and God knows what else? I've known you forever, Jane and I swear you look as great in your sixties as you did when you were a young woman. Does Joseph ever comment on that?"

"Never. As long as the house is clean and meals are on time, and I don't complain about being too tired for sex, he thinks life is hunky dory. If I confided in him the ways I've learned to save money, he would cut back my household allowance."

When the boys were toddlers, the family used to listen to the radio Saturday evenings. Jane would get out her knitting basket, Joseph would look annoyed, and say something like, "Do I have to listen to the clicking of those damn needles all through this program?" She never bothered to answer him, ignored his scowling face, and kept on knitting.

Their Sunday routine never varied. While Joseph got into his good suit in preparation for his weekly restaurant breakfast with his building cronies, Jane got herself and the boys ready for church.

Jane's faith was another taboo subject. Joseph dismissed going to church as a waste of time. When Harry turned twelve, Joseph announced that Harry was to be part of the Sunday morning breakfasts. He said he wanted Harry to begin to learn the business and the sooner, the better. Jane found it hard to forgive Joseph for ending Harry's church attendance. She encouraged Harry to be part of the youth activities in their church, but by the time he was sixteen, he was so immersed in the business, he spent practically every minute he wasn't in school with his father. Jane knew that Joseph was paying Harry a good wage, and had Harry totally committed to socking away every cent of it.

One time, when Harry was about twenty, she said to him, "Harry, you're what the girls call a handsome hunk.

How come you don't date very often?"

He shrugged and answered. "Too busy, I guess."

"Sure it's not because you're too cheap to treat a girl to a movie and a meal out?"

He looked surprised. "When I do date, I only date girls who go dutch. Dad says all women look for is a good meal ticket plus anything else they can get out of a man."

Jane was offended at Joseph's words coming out of her son's mouth. She made sure it was going to be different for Joey. When he had his twelfth birthday, Joseph made the same Sunday breakfast offer to him.

Joey turned it down. "I'd rather go to church with Mom."

Joseph didn't insist at first. He was more subtle than that. He offered Joey an after school job with good pay. Joseph hit the roof the day he found out that Joey wasn't banking his full pay check as he had been instructed to.

Joey always bought Jane a treat on his pay day. A new magazine, a rose from the florist, a bag of the chocolate covered peanuts she loved so much.

One evening at supper Joseph asked about the single yellow rose on the table. "It's the dead of winter," he said to Jane. "How can you spend money on such foolishness? I'm damn sure the price of that rose would have bought a bag of flour."

Before she could say anything, Joey spoke up. "Yellow roses are Mom's favourite. I bought it for her."

When anger turned Joseph's face red, Jane reached out and put a hand on his shoulder. "Joseph, it's a single rose. He paid fifty cents for it."

"Well, that Goddamn fifty cents should be in his

Goddamn bank account!"

Joey said quietly, "I earned that money, Dad. I worked hard for it, and I think I can decide what to do with it."

Jane was grateful that Joseph wasn't a hitting or punching man. He had never touched either of the boys. His face, now dark as thunder, he got up and slammed away from the table.

"See what you've done, you stupid twit," Harry snarled at Joey. "Dad will fire you if you're going to spend your money on foolishness."

Jane spoke. "Harry dear, it's good to indulge in a little foolishness once in a while. That beautiful rose brought me pleasure. I appreciated Joey's thoughtfulness."

Harry got up from the table and, in a good imitation of his father, stomped out of the room.

Joseph fired Joey the next morning, telling him he could have the job back when he promised to bank his whole pay check.

Joey immediately got himself a paper route. He made good money and kept the spending and saving of it to himself.

The battle lines were drawn, and Joseph never missed an opportunity to point out to Joey how Harry was going to be on top of the heap while he was going to have to settle for a run-of-the-mill job.

Jane secretly encouraged Joey to plan on going to university. He was a top student, and she told him there wasn't anything he couldn't do once he made up his mind. She brought books about the power of positive thinking home from the library, cautioning him, "Don't let your brother or father see you reading these."

Joey finished high school with honors, and the offer of three scholarships. The day he told her he was thinking of studying theology she thought her heart was going to burst with happiness. He lifted her off the floor and swung her around. "Mom, I don't know if I'll made a good minister or not, but I'm sure going to try."

She started to laugh, and she laughed so hard, she had to sit down.

"What? What? What are you laughing at?"

"I'm picturing your father's face when you tell him you're going to study theology." They were still laughing when Joseph's car pulled into the yard. She made shooing motions with her hands. "We'll decide later on the time and place to break the news."

Joseph shrugged when Joey told him. "I'm not surprised," was his surly comment. He turned on Jane. "This is your doing. Wouldn't surprise me if he turned out to be one of those Nancy boys. Never get married. Never have any kids."

Joey got through university on scholarships and a part-time newspaper job. He was married at twenty-five, the father of three by the time he was thirty, and two years later was called to the largest congregation in town.

Harry didn't marry until a few months before his thirty-seventh birthday. He married the twice divorced daughter of one of the town's richest men. It was all Jane could do to put on a calm face at the wedding. Joseph had been ecstatic. All that money.

Jane put the finishing touches to the chocolate cake and phoned Sarah before she left for the hospital. She wanted to tell her that the back door would be open in case she arrived before Jane's return.

As it turned out, her visit to the hospital was a short one. Dr. Allen and Joey were waiting for her just inside the entrance. Joey put his arms around her. "He's gone, Mom. Ten minutes ago. When I phoned the house you had already left. I was here doing visiting rounds when Dr. Allen paged me."

Jane's mind went blank. She asked the first question that popped into her head. "Did your father say anything before he died?"

The doctor took her by the arm and started to lead her down the hall toward Joseph's room. "I told them not to move him until you got here."

She moved away as if his hand was burning her arm.

Joey spoke. "I'll take Mom to the cafeteria. We'll have a coffee while we wait for Harry."

When they got to the cafeteria, Joey took a long time fussing over making her comfortable and fixing her coffee.

She asked, "Did you have any trouble locating Harry?"

He shook his head.

"Joseph was anxious to see Harry. Something about papers to be signed. I'm sure your father knew he didn't have much time left." She was babbling. "For a man so in control of everything, he didn't have a smidgen of control these last few months. I think that was the worst part for him."

"Dad was agitated about some final instructions for Harry, beckoned me to move closer so he could whisper, told me to tell Harry that he was to be in charge now and to look after you. I asked him if he would like me to say a prayer."

"What did he say to that?"

"He told me that he would say his own prayers."

"That's the last thing he said? That he would say his own prayers?"

Joey put his coffee mug in front of his mouth as if trying to hide a smile. "Mom, the last thing he said was pretty funny."

"What was it? Tell me."

"He said, "All that Goddamn knitting, and she never once knit anything for me. Not even a pair of socks.""

She wished she had been there at that moment. She would have told Joseph, "I would have knit you something if you had asked me."

She saw Harry approach and she held out her arms to him.

Harry's face was crumpled, sad. Jane hugged him. "I'm so sorry, Harry. You were close to your dad." She stood back and looked up at him. He was over six feet tall, like Joseph. The same dark handsome face. He was so like the young Joseph she had loved.

She suddenly remembered how much she had loved Joseph so many years ago. She broke down and started to cry. *That's who I will mourn. My young Joseph.*

A week after the funeral, Jane and Sarah drove out of town to the Country Inn for lunch. When the waiter had taken their order, Jane said, "I have some things to tell you, and I couldn't do it on home turf. I'm sure I would start smashing china."

"Well, for God's sake, tell me."

The waiter arrived with the bottle of white wine Jane ordered. "The boys and I had our meeting with Joseph's lawyer," she told Sarah.

Jane waited until the wine was poured. "Drink up, old friend, and don't interrupt me until I finish. The lawyer began by telling us that Joseph had been torn between leaving his will as it had been for years, that was everything in my name, with everything to be divided equally between the boys at my death. That, or turning everything over to Harry to manage. Of course, Harry was to take good care of me. Joseph told his lawyer he didn't think I was capable of handling so much money. The will hadn't been changed."

Jane held up a hand when Sarah began to interrupt. She took a gulp of wine and continued. "The house is in my name, and in my bank account is the money from Joseph's life insurance policy. That alone will keep me in comfort the rest of my life. I expected to own the house free and clear, and that I would receive Joseph's life insurance. What I didn't expect was the amount of money Joseph left, money saved during the years we were married."

She reached across the table and grabbed one of Sarah's hands. "Sarah, he's left over four hundred thousand dollars in cash, besides stocks and bonds and the business!"

Before Sarah could respond, Jane said, her face fierce with anger, "We could have eaten fresh fruit. We could have eaten roast beef once in a while. We could have gone to movies, had a vacation. I could have bought some decent clothes. The boys could have gone to summer camp. Instead, we spent our whole lives wrangling over nickels and dimes. I had to fight for cocoa on the grocery list, for God's sake. Sarah, I hated Joseph for the way he chose for us to live, and when I found out how much money he left, I wanted to strangle him with my bare hands."

Jane stopped long enough to refill their wine glasses. "Sarah, I wish you could have seen Harry's face when he realized that everything is in my name."

"What in the world did he say?"

"At first he expected that I would just turn everything over for him to manage."

"Are you going to do that?"

"Of course not. Harry started to yell at me right there in the lawyer's office. "What the hell do you know about managing money? Not for one minute am I going to let you have a say in the business!" Then he turned on Joey. "I'll bet you're pleased about this foolishness. I suppose you have plans to get around Mom to donate Dad's hard-earned money to that damn church of yours. Well, forget that. I'll go to court before I let that happen."

"The lawyer told Harry that the will couldn't be changed, that I would be in charge of all decisions. Harry cooled down a bit when I told him that the business was his. He worked for it, and neither Joey nor I had any interest in it. I told them both that the money Joseph left would be divided between them after I died."

Sarah said, "Jane, that money is going to make trouble for you."

"The surprising thing is, Sarah, when I asked myself what I really want, the answer is I really want control of the money. The boys can wait for it. When Harry came over this morning to talk about the kind of headstone he wanted ordered for Joseph's grave, I thought of the poem about the towns people coming to the widow to ask her why she hadn't put up a monument to her husband. Her answer was, "He turned my heart to stone. That's all the stone he'll get from me."

Jane reached for the wine bottle. "I'm getting tipsy. If I have another glass, will you drive home?"

Sarah nodded. "Jane, I know you. You're already making plans."

"Right, and the first thing I'm going to do is to do something outrageously extravagant, hoping that wherever Joseph is he'll know I'm having a great old time with his money."

"Do you think you'll know how to be extravagant after all those years of having to pinch pennies?"

"Just watch me. Seems like the world is like a stack of unopened Christmas gifts. I'm going to have some fun. I helped to save it, and I'm going to enjoy spending it. After I indulge in some foolishness, I'll just get on with my life. It won't be that difficult. I've got my garden to tend to, and a stack of books to read." Jane held out her glass to her friend for a refill. "And I've got some mourning to do."

TELL ME
EVERYTHING

My brother and I live on opposite coasts. I visit him for a week every spring. It seems like a miracle to me, boarding a plane in Sydney on a spring day that had yet to experience winter's last fling, dull skies, a chilly wind, buds barely showing, and the need for a warm coat, then, to step off the plane in Vancouver to the sight of trees in full leaf. Then the drive to my brother's home, down streets lined with cherry trees with their gorgeous blossoms, yards full of daffodils and tulips.

The occasion this time was Roy's fiftieth birthday. On the second day of the visit we were sitting outside, drinking our after-dinner coffee and enjoying the warmth of the spring evening.

Roy's wife, Marnie, was showing signs of boredom. I was winding up my story about Uncle Bert's trip to England. Marnie was stifling a yawn.

I gave Roy the look that said, "Enough family talk", and turned to Marnie. I said, "The roast beef dinner was delicious, Marnie. I'd like to help with the meals while I'm here."

I knew full well she wouldn't let me help. The truth was she wouldn't even let me put the morning coffee on. Her kitchen was out of bounds to me.

I was used to Marnie's coolness toward me, but then she hadn't warmed up to any of Roy's family. She had made it clear from the very beginning that travelling to Nova Scotia to visit us was not high on her list.

The first summer Roy brought her home, they had been married for six months and she was pregnant. The family threw a joint wedding and baby shower for her in our little church hall. There was a big turnout. Everyone in town liked Roy and wanted to welcome his wife. Marnie sat on the be-ribboned chair looking embarrassed. She didn't crack a smile the whole evening. As soon as the gifts were opened, she said she had a terrible headache and would Roy please take her home. She didn't even stay for a cup of tea.

My sisters were fit to be tied. We had hoped that Roy would marry a down-home girl and settle in Nova Scotia. Our oldest sister, who was the one who organized the evening, looked let down as she folded the gift paper. We did our best to give Marnie a good, Nova Scotia welcome. We hadn't quite pulled it off.

I have to admit I felt sorry for her the evening of the shower. She was in a place very different from her home in

Vancouver. She was newly married, pregnant, and surrounded by a clan of boisterous Cape Bretoners.

Marnie thanked me for the compliment about the roast-beef dinner. She added, "Roy says no one cooks roast beef the way his mother cooked it."

Roy laughed, "I might have said that once or twice." "Once or twice!" she snapped at him. "You've got a short memory." She turned her back on us and started to tidy the flower pots.

"Tell me more about Gail's new home," I said quickly. Their daughter Gail was a safe topic. Marnie could talk endlessly about Gail's success as a fashion model. Gail's perfect husband. Gail's new home. More spacious and far superior to theirs.

She stood up. She looked like a model herself. Bone thin. Blonde hair tied back in a pony tail. Designer jeans. It was hard to believe she was forty-five. I knew what was coming next. Time for her to find some necessary chores to do. Time to escape the down-home talk.

"I'm going to do a few gardening chores out front while there's still some light," she said as she walked away.

She and Roy kept a beautiful garden. Working together in the garden was the one time during my visits they seemed relaxed.

When Marnie left us, I turned to Roy. "Roy, can you explain why Marnie never wants to come East?"

He said he didn't want to talk about it.

Marnie had been an only child. Her parents died when she was in her teens. I could understand why she was uncomfortable in the big noisy crowd that made up our family.

Roy and I sat sipping our coffee. He finally broke the silence. "Tell me about Eve."

Here we go, I thought. The questions about Eve were always the same. "Have you seen her lately? How does she look? Is she well? Does her marriage seem O.K.?"

My answers were always vague. Eve's sister, Joan, was my best friend so I knew all the details of Eve's unhappy life. I didn't see any point in telling Roy that Ian was an abusive husband, that they were both drinking too much, that their grown son was always in some kind of trouble.

Roy went inside for the coffee pot. When he returned, he said, "Come on, Sis. You must have some news of Eve."

"Roy," I grumbled, "I travel west every year to visit you. You never come home anymore. If you came home for a visit you could see Eve for yourself." I added. "Anyway, Roy, the past is the past. Never mind Eve. You have three sisters who would be thrilled to have you home for a visit."

"The few times Marnie and I did go home for a visit, Eve was always away somewhere. Do you think that was deliberate?"

"I haven't a clue, Roy," I lied. I wanted to tell him, *She didn't want you to see how she's changed.*

He stared into his coffee mug. "I don't feel the pull, now that Mom and Dad are gone. Besides, Marnie prefers to go somewhere else on our holidays."

I wanted to chew him out the way I used to when he was ten and I was twenty. I wanted to ask him, "Couldn't Marnie come east with you once in a while? Didn't he think they were both selfish never coming for a visit?" I wanted to ask him, "Is there some reason you can't board a plane by yourself?" I had decided to quit coaxing him to come home some time ago. I became tired of the coaxing.

He held out his hands to me. "Sis, you're right. It's time I went home for a visit. He rubbed his eyes with his knuckles. "Does turning fifty make one nostalgic about the past?"

Stretching out his long legs, he closed his eyes and began to talk as if he were sitting there by himself. "I remember how Dad used to call Eve his Bonny Lass. God, wasn't she beautiful? That gorgeous red hair. Those soft brown eyes. I think about her every time I see a woman with red hair. I wonder what my life would be like if I had married her."

I thought of the part the family had in preventing Roy from running to Eve's rescue.

"Don't talk daft, Roy," I said. "You were nineteen years old. Your first year of university. Your whole life ahead of you."

His face had old memories written all over it. "I really loved her. I didn't care that she was pregnant by Ian. He got her drunk, you know."

I couldn't look at him. It hurt to see him still thinking about Eve.

We heard Marnie approach and he said abruptly, "Tell me more about King George School being torn down."

Marnie moved toward the coffee tray. "Have you managed to get some news of your childhood sweetheart?"

His voice was cold. "Actually, we've been talking about the possibility of my going home for a visit."

"Not bloody likely," she said. "I've already told you I want to go to England for our holidays this year."

"You'll have a good a time without me." He stood up and moved toward the kitchen door. "I'm going to try to book a seat on Sis's flight." He gave me a quick smile. "You wouldn't mind the company, would you?"

When he was gone, Marnie threw her coffee mug against the brick wall of the house. She just sat there and stared at the broken pottery, holding back tears. Then she turned to me. "This has been coming for some time. Even with all that distance, you people manage to keep him tied to you."

I didn't want to listen. I started to go inside and she reached out and touched me. "Dorothy, please. I'm sorry." She began picking up the broken pieces of mug. "I don't want Roy going east without me. Please ask him if I can join you."

I didn't know what to say. Finally, I said, "I'll go in and tell him to book you a seat too." I headed for the kitchen where I could see Roy was talking on the phone. He nodded, his face expressionless, when I told him Marnie was coming with us. Then I went upstairs to the guest room. My head was aching. I took two aspirins and stretched out on the bed. I felt trapped in the over-flowered guestroom. I thought about home and how glad I would be to get back to my own bed.

Roy will want to see Eve. How was he going to re-act when I tell the truth about Eve's marriage? I decided I would tell the two of them about Eve's sad life on the flight home. It didn't seem fair not to tell Roy.

The look on Marnie's face when Roy told her he was going East just about broke my heart. Then I reminded myself Roy's marriage was none of my business.

I made plans to make Marnie feel welcome. We won't bowl her over with parties and invitations everywhere. I'll suggest some places she might like to see, and for sure, we'll drive around the Cabot Trail. I'll begin by going downstairs to tell her I'm happy that she's coming home with us.

ALTHEA'S VISIT

nne was remembering the story her friend Mary had told her a few days ago.

"It was the first time I bathed Mother's feet," Mary said. "As you know, I looked after her totally that last month. Her feet were almost as worn as her hands. Washing those feet and remembering what a hard life she had led, I was suddenly able to lay down all the bitter stuff between us. You know what a stormy relationship we had. My taking care of her became loving, not a sham, as I had expected it to be."

Anne patted her own mother's feet gently. Laura snapped at her, "For God's sake, Anne, my feet are dry! What's making you so slow this morning?"

Anne sprinkled talcum on Laura's feet and reached for the pale blue slippers. "You have beautiful feet, Mother."

Laura gave a snort. "Well, let's leave them bare and put them on display for our company this afternoon."

Anne grinned. She was picturing her sister Althea's face if she were to find their mother barefooted.

Anne went to the closet for the requested housecoat. Laura's housecoats were more like old-fashioned tea gowns. She was vain about her appearance and Anne encouraged that vanity.

On her monthly visit, Althea acted as if the Saturday drive she and her husband made from Baddeck to Sydney Mines was a sacrifice.

Anne knew that after spending an hour with their mother, Althea and Gerald would head for their usual Saturday activity, attending antique shops, on the prowl for yet another perfect acquisition for their perfect Victorian house.

A year ago, after Laura's stroke, Anne had insisted on Laura giving up her apartment. Anne converted her den into a bedroom for herself, papered the walls of the one bedroom in her apartment with a pale yellow flowered paper. She stored her bedroom suite so that Laura could have her own mahogany suite in the newly papered room. Having beautiful things around her had been important to her mother her whole life.

Althea had pushed for a nursing home. She disapproved of Laura's moving in with Anne. "You're as stubborn as she is," Althea had said to Anne. "You two have never been able to get along. How are you going to manage living with each other?" Anne glanced at her watch. "I had better set the table," she said to Laura. "The vegetarians have requested a salad and herbal tea for lunch."

"Aren't you going to brush my hair?"

"Mother, there's nothing wrong with your arms. The exercise will do you good." She gave her mother's soft white curls a pat and headed for the kitchen.

The visit had the sameness of all of Althea and Gerald's visits. Flowers and a box of candy. The telling of their comings and goings. The bragging about their only child, Leah, who was studying law.

Hearing about Leah was the only part of the conversation that interested Anne. She doted on her niece, and wondered how those two stuffed shirts had ever produced such an enchanting young woman.

After lunch, Gerald wheeled Laura's wheel chair into the living room while Anne and Althea went into the kitchen to wash the dishes. Anne hated that part of the visit. She and her sister usually found something to argue about. This time it was the Limoges china. "I can't help wondering," Althea began, "why you used the Limoges to serve a simple salad."

"I thought you liked eating off the Limoges."

"I do, but it's a little ostentatious for lunch." Althea dried a saucer carefully. "Don't forget, Mother's promised the Limoges to me."

"How can I forget? You remind me at least once a month."

"Anne, have you spoken to mother about the specifics of her will? I really want Leah to have Mother's bedroom suite."

Anne threw down the dish cloth. *God, this sister of mine makes me crazy, she's so focused on things.* Anne exploded.

"Why don't you have Mother move in with you? She'd have her few possessions with her and then you'd be able to control what happens to them when she dies."

Althea said nothing.

"By the way," Anne continued, "you said you were going to invite Mother to stay with you for a few days. Have you decided when?"

Althea turned to face her. "You're putting me on the defensive again. You're trying to make me feel guilty. Gerald and I lead very busy lives. We have social responsibilities you couldn't begin to understand."

Anne closed her eyes. *God, I hope I'm not going to get the speech about my being single, and therefore free to look after Mother. Managing a clothing store and running a household doesn't take up any of my time, of course.*

Anne took a deep breath in an effort to calm down. "Althea, I'm not asking this for myself. Mother feels hurt that you don't invite her for a visit. You know how much she would enjoy a change of scene."

Althea pointed to the clock on the stove. "My God, it's two o'clock. I promised Gerald we would leave at two."

"I'm sure the antique shops will still be open when you begin your hunt."

Althea carefully folded the apron she had borrowed. Her voice was full of hurt. "Gerald is always very good about driving me here to visit Mother every month. Going shopping with him is the least I can do in exchange."

"Althea, get out of my sight before I really lose it and kick your fat rump," Anne warned through clenched teeth.

"Don't you dare speak to me like that, Anne. I swear you're becoming downright common."

"And you're becoming more and more self-centred. But why should that surprise me?"

When they were gone Anne threw herself on the couch and looked across the living room at her mother.

Laura's head was back, her eyes closed. "They stayed five minutes past the allotted time. You missed Gerald's twitching." She started to laugh. "To think how I used to be thrilled about Althea marrying a successful business man. Have you ever met such a colossal bore?"

Anne said, "They deserve each other."

"You're right. That's one bloody mutual admiration society. All they ever talk about is themselves."

"Anything else bothering you, Ma?"

"Oh, the sameness of the visits, and the fact that I've been with you for a year now and not once have they mentioned taking me to their place for a visit." There was a pause and a loud, sad, sigh. "You know Anne, dear, I always thought Althea would be the one who would take care of me if ever i needed taking care of. You and I were always so prickly with each other."

Laura looked close to tears. Anne got up and moved toward the liquor cabinet. "Is it too early in the day for a good, stiff drink?"

"Best idea I've heard all day." Laura banged on the arms of her chair. "Before you make the drinks, do something for me. Take those damn, boring mums down the hall to Mrs. MacDonald. She hasn't a soul to do anything nice for her and she loves flowers."

As Anne reached for the flowers, her mother grabbed one of her hands and kissed it. "Mrs. MacDonald isn't as fortunate as I am. She doesn't have you for a daughter."

THE FUNERAL

The Deans lived in the other half of our miner's double house. Every kid in the neighbourhood loved Mr. Dean, but was scared to death of Mrs.Dean. She had a scary face and a piercing sharp voice. I never went into her store when she was there. I used to peek in the window and if I saw skinny Mrs. Dean in her long black dress, her white hair wrapped in a tight braid around her head, I put my pennies away for another time.

I liked to buy my penny candy when Mr. Dean or their daughter Carrie was minding the store.

After Mr. Dean died and Carrie married, Mrs. Dean was more miserable than ever with the kids who came in. My mother made excuses for her, said she was like that because she was old and unhappy.

Mr.Dean had built the small store when he had to leave the pit because of lung trouble. The neighbours pitched in with the heavy work. The last few years of Mr. Dean's life were spent tending the store. Everyone loved Mr.Dean, especially us kids when he gave us extra big scoops of ice-cream.

My dad said that Mr. Dean had the largest funeral he ever attended. When Mrs. Dean died only two years after Mr. Dean, the first thing I thought was, *I bet there won't be a crowd at her funeral.*

The day before Mrs. Dean's funeral, my mother had me standing on a kitchen chair pinning up the hem of a dress, a dress to wear to the funeral. It was navy blue, made of soft silky material. I liked it, but then I liked most of the hand-me-downs I got from my cousin Margaret.

"Stand still, for God's sake," my mother ordered. She and Aunt Em were talking about the funeral. I liked listening to the conversations my mother had with her sister. I found out lots of things listening to them. Grown ups never gave kids information they needed. They said things like, "When you're older you'll know all about it." Kids need to know things when they're kids.

Aunt Em stuffed toast and strawberry jam in her mouth, took a swig of tea and kept on talking. "Dying in your sleep has got to be the most peaceful death. I wonder what Carrie will do about the house and the store?"

My mother put the last pin in the hem and pulled the dress over my head. "The old bat left a long list of instructions for Carrie. Told her to sell everything and give the proceeds to the Presbyterian Church."

Aunt Em laughed and gave my mother a shove. "How's

that for getting back at Carrie for marrying a Roman Catholic?"

My mother poured more tea and gave me one of her endless orders. "As soon as you're dressed, wash up the breakfast dishes. And brush your hair before you leave for school."

As I did what I was told, I thought about Carrie and her husband Donald. I was forever trying to figure out grown-ups. I made a solemn vow to myself that when I grew up and had kids I would explain everything to them. They wouldn't even have to ask me. I'd just tell them everything they needed to know.

Carrie married Donald shortly after her father died. They met when she bought a 1933 car from his dealership in Waterford. It was a funny courtship because Mrs. Dean wouldn't allow Carrie to invite Donald home. Every Saturday afternoon Carrie used to drive over to Waterford, returning home late Sunday evening.

Mrs. Dean refusing to welcome Donald into her home surprised no one. It amazed everyone that Carrie, an old-maid school teacher, had a serious beau, and that she was standing up to her mother.

Carrie and Donald had a quiet wedding at the Roman Catholic Church in Waterford. My mother's younger sister, Ruth, was Carrie's bridesmaid, so I got to hear every detail of the wedding and all about Carrie and Donald's new house. Ruth called it "a darling little cottage."

Carrie and Donald bought the house three months before they were married. They spent every weekend painting and papering and fixing it up. Mrs. Dean refused to visit the new house. She also refused to attend the wedding.

Carrie gave up her teaching job. Just as well. Besides a husband and house to look after, she had to drive to the Bay three afternoons a week so she could help her mother with the store and the housework.

I liked the days when Carrie was in the store. She would come to our back door and invite me in for a visit with her. Carrie was a great one for surprise treats.

What I used to try and figure out was why Mrs. Dean was so mean to Carrie. She sure didn't treat her the way I thought a daughter should be treated.

The day I asked my mother to explain this to me she gave me a hug and said, "You'll understand more about grown-ups when you're a grown-up yourself." No help at all.

The morning of the funeral, Carrie and my Aunt Ruth sat in our kitchen, drinking coffee and going over old Mrs. Dean's funeral arrangements.

Aunt Ruth asked her, "Are you really going to follow those instructions? You don't have to, you know. They aren't set up legal." I sat there, quiet as a mouse. I didn't want to miss a thing. Most of the time, Carrie had a calm, coping kind of manner. That day she was far from calm. The rims of her eyes were a permanent pink and her voice was sad. "Mamma made me promise. What can I do?"

Aunt Ruth refilled their cups. "Read that thing to me again."

"A closed casket. No eulogy. One hymn. "Abide with Me". At the end of the hymn the minister is to announce that proceeds from the sale of her house and store are to be used for the maintenance of the church camp for children. No food and drink after the burial." Carrie put the list down and reached for the tissue box.

My mother had come into the room while Carrie was reading. She told Carrie, "My fridge and cupboards are stuffed to the hilt with sandwiches, cakes and pies. "Your mother's instructions didn't say anything about a cup of tea and bite to eat in this house. Donald said he would see to some beer and liquor."

Carrie started to cry again. "Thank you so much. Many of our Waterford friends are coming to the funeral. It would be so embarrassing not to be able to offer them a cup of tea."

At our house after the funeral service, I heard my dad tell my mother that he got the surprise of his life when he saw how many people were at the church.

My mother said, "Probably attended for Carrie's sake. Thank God it's a fine day. People will be able to sit outside on lawn chairs."

She and my dad were in the kitchen refilling the ice bucket. He reached for one of the ice cubes, rubbed it on her lips and gave her a kiss.

"What are you smiling about?" she asked him.

"About the contingent of Roman Catholics in the Presbyterian Church today. Do you suppose Mrs. Dean is already spinning in her grave?"

When they noticed me standing there listening, my mother held out the full ice bucket. "Get this to your Aunt Ruth." Carrie and Donald stayed at our house overnight. When Donald left for Waterford the next morning Carrie asked me if I would help her do some sorting. The contents of the house had been left to her and she had to decide what she would keep and what she would sell.

Carrie was sitting in the kitchen rocker when I joined her. She was holding a little brown cuckoo clock in her lap and crying quietly. She pointed to the wall where you could see the faint shape of the clock on the flowered wallpaper. "Larry gave Mamma this clock for her birthday the summer he was ten and I was twelve. Five days before he drowned."

Carrie stood up and carefully placed the clock back up on the wall. "It was July and Larry was attending Church camp."

I knew she had a brother who died when he was little. When I asked my mother about him, she told me to be quiet and never mention Larry's name in front of Mrs. Dean. As if I would ever have the nerve to mention anything to Mrs. Dean.

My head was spinning with questions. "Will you hang that cuckoo clock in your kitchen?"

"I don't think so, dear. It's too sad a reminder of Larry."

She grabbed my hands. "Oh, my dear, I wish you had known Mamma before Larry died. She was so full of fun then."

"But what about you and Mr. Dean? You lost him too."

"Yes, we lost him too, but Father and I eventually dealt with the pain. Mamma just didn't know how to do that. She lived for Larry, and when he was gone, she was never the same."

Carrie reached up for the clock and pressed it against her cheek. "I think I'll take Larry's clock home with me after all." She led me out of the kitchen and into the dining room. "Help me sort out the china." She gave me a sweet smile. "And you can ask me the questions that are written all over your face."

I told her, "The thing I want to know is, why don't grown-ups explain important things to kids?"

THE MISSING PHOTOGRAPH

When Connie met Mike, she knew he was the man she was going to marry. That was an unusual thought for down-to-earth, practical Connie to have.

On the evening of their second date, when they were saying goodnight at her Aunt Em's front door, Mike told her he knew that they were going to spend the rest of their lives together.

They met at a Sydney YMCA dance. Mike was one of the hundreds of men just returning home at the end of the war. The YMCA was once again overcrowded.

It was the first dance of the evening. Mike walked across the dance floor to where Connie stood, talking to a girlfriend. He asked her to dance. She knew he was just the best looking guy in the room with more than one girl in town crazy about him. She remembered thinking, *my God, Mike Thompson is asking me for a dance.* Connie had been in high school the year Mike went overseas. She remembered exactly what it felt like the moment he held out his arms and she walked into them.

They didn't leave the dance floor the rest of the evening. Between numbers they just stood there, looking at each other, saying hardly a word. The band would start up and Mike would hold out his arms again. Connie was only vaguely aware that there were other dancers on the floor.

He asked her if he could walk her home. She told him she had come to the dance with a girlfriend. He said, "Then I'll walk you both home."

At her Aunt's front door he asked if he could take her to the YMCA Christmas formal the coming weekend.

The next morning, Mike called just as Aunt Em and Connie were leaving for church. He said, "I can't bear the thoughts of not seeing you until Saturday night. Would you like to go for a drive this evening? Find a nice place to have dinner?"

Connie said, "Yes. I'd like that." Her heart would say yes to anything he wanted.

She didn't hear a word of the sermon that Sunday morning. She just sat there on the hard pew, counting the hours before she would see him again.

After dinner that evening they went for a walk. The air was so clear, so cold, the snow crunchy underfoot. There were Christmas wreaths and candles in the windows of the houses they walked past. One house was so beautifully decorated they stopped for a minute to admire it. Mike squeezed her hand. "Someday, we'll have a home like that, Connie."

It all sounds romantically corny now, but it's exactly how their life together began. After that evening they were inseparable. They talked endlessly about all the things they wanted to do with their lives.

Like many returning servicemen, Mike decided he wanted more education. He registered for the winter semester at Nova Scotia Tech in Halifax, so that after mid-January they were together only on weekends.

There was never any question of her leaving Aunt Em and finding work in Halifax. Mike knew and understood Connie's commitment to her Aunt who had taken care of her after her parents' death when she was six years old.

Their plan was to get married in two years. Mike encouraged Connie's dreams about going to Teachers' College. Her wanting to become an elementary school teacher was as important to him as his wanting to become an architect.

Connie was more than a little nervous the first time she met Mike's mother. The truth was she had never been so nervous in her life. She felt overwhelmed, sitting at the huge mahogany table, in the formal dining room, concentrating on using the right silver, trying to sound intelligent. The evening was not a success.

The worst part of the evening was after dinner. Mike made the suggestion that he and Connie do the dishes.

"No," his mother said. "I'll wash. You and Connie may dry and re-set the table for me. I'm having a dinner party tomorrow night."

Her face said, "A real dinner party. Not just this little dinner to please my son."

When they were done setting the table, Mrs. Thompson handed Connie a pair of rubber gloves and a scouring pad. "You can take over. I have some things to do in the dining room."

Connie automatically reached for the kitchen shears and cut the new soap pad in two.

Mrs. Thompson stared at her. "Why on earth did you do that?"

"We always cut soap pads in two," Connie stammered. "Makes the box go further."

Mike's mother gave her a condescending look that said, "I forgot that you're poor."

Mike laughed and said, "We all have our little economies, Mother. For instance, I know a lady who is obsessed about turning out lights."

"That," she said with a sniff, "was a wartime necessity."

When his mother left the room Mike grabbed Connie and gave her a big hug. "It's over, Darling. The first time is over." He started to laugh again. "Not that Saturday night dinners with Mother will ever be something you'll relish. But you'll learn how to handle it as I do. Smile a lot. Eat the good food and think about what we're going to do with the rest of the evening. And speaking of that, let's hurry and finish up here. We're going dancing."

"Mike, I can tell your mother doesn't like me. She doesn't think I'm good enough for you. Your mother is never going to like me."

He stopped her by putting his mouth over hers. They were thirty seconds into the kiss when his mother returned to the kitchen. The look of dismissal she had given Connie earlier turned into something else. Connie had never seen such intense displeasure on a face before. Connie thought, *No matter what Mike says, I know his mother is never going to like me. And I know in my gut that dealing with this woman is going to be a lifetime challenge for me.*

When Mike went away to Halifax they wrote each other every day, and they lived for the weekends.

Mike's mother made no attempt to see Connie again. That was fine with Connie.

Two months after the first dinner fiasco, Connie was invited again. An old girlfriend of Mike's was in town for the weekend. At first Connie wasn't included, but Mike told his mother there was no possibility of his being there without Connie.

Connie refused at first, but the hurt look on Mike's face, and her own curiosity got the better of her.

Getting ready, she was more anxious than she had been the first time. Connie had two good dresses. That evening she wore Mike's favourite, the blue one. The first time he saw it he said, "I love that dress on you. It's the same beautiful shade of blue as your eyes."

Connie would have loved to be able to buy some new clothes, but it took every cent of her salary at the bookshop, plus Aunt Em's small pension to buy the groceries and run their small house.

Her anxiety hit a new high as she dressed and thought about this old girlfriend of Mike's. He told her they had been childhood friends, that they had dated in high school, that Claire had gone away to study music while he attended the local Business College. At that time Mike had planned to join his father in the family insurance business.

A few months after Mike began the course in Business Administration, his father died of a heart attack. Six months later the war began and Mike joined up.

Mike talked little about his years overseas, but one evening he told Connie about the English girl he had been in love with. They were exchanging their views on sex and talking about their sexual experiences. Connie didn't have much to tell because she was one of the cautious virgins of the forties.

When Mike told her about his overseas love affair, she felt sad for him. The girl he had the affair with had been in love with someone else.

"What about Claire?" she asked him. "Didn't you two ever fool around?"

He looked embarrassed. "Claire wanted to. Not because we were in love. We were never in love. She said she was just tired of being a virgin."

Connie teased him. "How come you turned down such a generous offer?"

His answer was, "I wasn't in love with her."

Connie's heart did a flip-flop when they arrived at Mike's home and she was introduced to Claire. She was one of the most beautiful women Connie had ever seen. She was Mike's exact height, five eleven. They both had blonde, wavy hair. They could have passed for brother and sister.

Ida Thompson was in her glory. She looked handsome in her newly permed white hair, her navy silk dress and pearls. She presided over the dinner table like a queen. Connie felt like the Little Match Girl let in from the cold. Of course Claire was the Princess in the Princess and the

Pea.

Connie was quieter than usual that evening, letting the animated conversation about Claire's music career float over her head. She played with the roast beef on her plate. The time before she had explained to Mrs. Thompson that she rarely ate red meat. Connie thought it was interesting that roast beef was being served again.

Mike's mother was a superb cook. With the help of her cleaning lady, the house looked as if someone important would be arriving any minute. Her famous African violets were displayed everywhere. They were always in bloom, but then, Connie thought, they wouldn't dare not be in bloom.

Driving her home, Mike said, "Darling, you were awfully quiet tonight."

"True."

"Mother did go on and on about Claire's accomplishments, didn't she?" He heaved a great sigh. "Poor Claire. She's had to put up with mother's match making since kindergarten."

The following morning Claire phoned Connie. "I know you must be getting ready for church, but I'm taking the noon train and I wanted to have a quick chat with you."

Connie made a hesitating sound.

"Connie, Mike phoned me early this morning and asked me to go for a walk with him. He and his mother had an awful row last night after he took you home. He wanted to talk about it."

Connie's only reaction was to clear her throat. She didn't know what to say.

"Before I say anything else, I have to tell you that I

think you're the perfect girl for Mike. I've never seen him so happy."

She continued, "I don't know what Mike's mother has told you, but Mike and I have never been serious about each other. I'm calling to tell you to be careful. Ida Thompson is a very controlling woman. She's always been very jealous of any girl Mike's been the least bit interested in."

"I assume she wasn't jealous of you."

"That's because she chose me. I think she thought that gave her a kind of control. Connie, do be careful."

"What do you mean?"

She rushed on. "She was waiting for Mike last night with a litany of complaints. You're too thin, too poor, no social background, etc. etc."

Claire continued, "Mike told her if she persisted in being negative about you that she would be seeing little of him after your wedding, not to mention her future grand-children. He told her that it was about time she realized that she couldn't run his life."

"Oh God," was all Connie could say.

Claire said good-bye. "Remember, Connie, be careful. Ida adores Mike. He's her only child and in a way, her whole life. She could make a lot of trouble for you."

Later in the day when Mike and Connie went for their Sunday walk, he told her about the quarrel, and about his calling Claire.

"Clair knows Mother and her manipulating almost as well as I do, and I wanted to get the quarrel off my chest before I told you about it."

"Claire called me this morning, Mike," she told him.

"And I've been thinking all day about the things she

said. I've decided that I'm going to have to live with your mother's disapproval of me. I'm not going to go out of my way to try and win her over. Do you mind?"

Mike stopped and held her face in his hands. His voice was full of worry. "The thing is Connie, I'm afraid she'll interfere in some God-awful way, change how you feel about me. It's asking a lot, my asking you to put up with her."

"Well, it does hurt that she isn't even trying to get to know me."

"Darling, that doesn't matter. You're going to be my wife!" Then he grabbed her and hugged her. "God, why are we waiting so long to get married? I can't stand not being with you."

A few days later something happened that made Connie distrust Mike's mother even more. She had come home from work bone tired. Aunt Em had made a pot of her wonderful bean soup for supper and hot apple pie for dessert.

Connie polished off the last crumb of her pie before asking Aunt Em what was troubling her.

"How do you know something is troubling me?"

"Because your forehead is puckered the way it gets when something is bothering you. That's how I know."

"My friend Hilda came by for tea this afternoon."

"And?"

"She said something that made me angry."

"What did Hilda say?"

"Ida Thompson told Hilda's sister that Mike is often attracted to lame ducks."

Connie gave Aunt Em a hug. "We're going to ignore that. We're not going to let that woman spoil things for us."

Connie patted the pocket that had held Mike's daily letter. She had read it in the usual hurry when she first got in from work. Now it was time to have a second cup of tea and re-read it, reading bits of it aloud to Aunt Em. That ritual had become the best part of her work day.

Her twenty-first birthday fell on a Saturday in March. Mike had asked her to go dancing after dinner at his mother's.

By this time Mike's mother had taken a different tack with Connie. The disdain was replaced with a cool but civilized formality.

At times Connie felt a twinge of pity for her. She could see how difficult it was for Ida to smile when Mike brought her home.

Mike held her hand constantly or had an arm around her shoulders. Every once in a while, when Mike wasn't looking, she saw Ida look at their closeness. Connie saw her lips tighten in disapproval.

When they were eating dessert that evening, Ida passed a large, beautifully wrapped box to Connie. "I thought this would be a suitable gift. Something for your cedar chest."

In the box was a white damask table cloth and eight matching napkins. Connie thought, *she knows damn well I don't have a cedar chest. The pillow cases and luncheon cloths Aunt Em is busy embroidering are stored in a bottom dresser drawer.*

"It's a beautiful gift. Thank you very much." Connie said.

She still hadn't come to the place where she could call her Ida. She couldn't even call her Mrs. Thompson. She knew in her heart she could never call her Mother. Maybe when she and Mike had children she would call her Grandma.

Mike passed her a flat box, the size of a photograph, and that's what it was, a beautiful black and white photograph.

"You're wearing that Joseph Cotton look," Connie told him. Her eyes filled with tears when she read what he had written in the corner. "To my dearest darling with all my love."

Ida stood up. She turned on Mike. "I've been asking you to have a photo taken for me ever since you returned from overseas. Your high school graduation photo is outdated and I told you so a dozen times."

Without another word she stomped upstairs.

Later, when they had finished the dishes and were ready to leave for the dance, Ida refused to come down to say good-bye. That birthday gift from Mike sealed her fate with Ida.

Connie knew they would never be friends.

The life Mike and Connie planned for themselves, turned out to be, with the exception of Mike's mother never accepting Connie, everything they planned when they were young and full of dreams.

They had two wonderful daughters, successful careers, a beautiful home, good friends. Mike and Connie remained crazy in love with each other from the first day to the last.

Connie was grateful that Aunt Em had lived long enough to see them married, and to be with them when the girls were born. Aunt Em died when Joanie was six months old.

Mike died of a heart attack a week after his fiftieth birthday. Connie was forty-two, Emma seventeen and Joanie fifteen. Ida was seventy when Mike died. She was quietly stoic during that sad time. She helped Connie run the house for a while after the funeral. She was wonderful with the girls. She had always doted on them and did everything she could to help them deal with their father's death. Connie appreciated Ida's competence and support.

The day Mike's photograph went missing Connie knew Ida had taken it. She didn't have an ounce of proof but she just knew Ida had taken the photograph.

Ida had been coming to the house every day, insisting on doing housework and cooking meals. Connie knew that the constant washing out of cupboards and dusting every surface in the house was her rebuke to Connie's casual approach to housekeeping.

When Connie told Ida that she didn't want her doing the house cleaning, Ida made a long speech about how exhausted Connie looked after a day of teaching. In truth it was the teaching that helped Connie stay sane.

When Ida was asked about the missing photograph she said it had likely been misplaced. Connie told her it had never been off her bedside table in all the years she and Mike had been married. Ida shrugged.

Connie stared at her mother-in-law and thought, *When you die, I will sift through your belongings and find Mike's photograph.*

One Saturday, about six months after the photograph went missing, Connie decided she wasn't going to wait until Ida died to get the photograph back. Ida and the girls were shopping. She decided it would be a good time to make the search.

She found it in the first place she looked, under one of

the pillows on Ida's bed. Connie cried when she saw the photograph. She hugged it to her and hurried home.

She thought, *Ida and the girls will soon be home. I'll make some cookies and put a pot of coffee on.*

That evening, when Ida settled herself in bed she reached under the pillow for the journal she kept there. She wrote, *I coveted that photograph. I had to have it. The photograph was a comfort to me.*

After my darling son died, I had to stay healthy for the girls. They needed me. Connie looked like she was heading for a nervous breakdown. The doctor had her on sleeping pills for months. I was sure I would end up looking after the house and the girls for a long time.

At that time, I did have some compassion for Connie, even though she was never a really suitable wife for Mike. She was never good enough for him. She had no background to speak of, no social skills. She insisted on getting her teachers' license and teaching. She should have stayed home and taken better care of the girls and the house.

One day when she came home from school, the girls were helping me prepare dinner. "Now, dears," I was telling them, "try to make your mother relax and have a drink before dinner. She isn't strong, you know. Try to convince her to go to bed right after dinner.

"She must have heard me because she came flying into the kitchen and slammed her books on the table. "Grandma, I want you to stop implying that I'm some kind of an invalid.

Connie told her, "You've got to stop hovering. A friend told me that you've been telling people that I'm on pills and that I'm unable to take care of the house." She added, "I won't have you treat me as if I were a basket case. Mike wouldn't want it. Mike would not want you to coddle the girls either, or for us to act as if our lives are going to be forever one long mourning."

When Connie said that to me, I thought. "When you're old, you'll find out, my girl. You'll find out what life is like without a husband. Mike won't be here to protect you. You'll find out."

Today she found the photograph. She had sent the girls and me out to do the grocery shopping. When we got back she had cookies and coffee for us on a tray in the living room.

I had taken my first sip of coffee when I saw the photograph on the fire place mantle.

I almost fainted. "You found the photograph," I said.

"Yes. I'm going to keep it in the living room from now on," she said. "We need Mike's photo with us. The girls and I need that photo of Mike to remind us every day that love never dies. It lasts forever".

Then she told me I was to stop my daily visits.

She said, "We will still have Saturday evenings together. And Emma and Joanie can spend as much time at your place as they want to."

My old heart sank. "I'm sorry," I stammered, knowing I wasn't sorry.

I could tell by the way she looked at me that she didn't believe me when I said I was sorry. She didn't trust me.

Just as I never trusted her.

She was always terribly jealous of how much Mike loved me. I know she's also jealous of how much the girls love me. Jealousy is a terrible thing.

BEDS AND ROSES

I love my bed. I read in bed every night of my life. That infuriates my husband. When I moved into the guest room, I did feel some twinges of guilt, but not enough to change my mind. God knows there were more contentious issues between us than my reading in bed, but it was the one I used as an excuse to get a bed of my own. That happened about five years after we had both retired and moved home to Cape Breton.

Tom assumed my sleeping in the guest room was a temporary arrangement. He sulked for the first week. That man's got sulking down to an art. I think of the years I did everything possible to cajole him out of a sulk, or out of an angry fit, or out of giving me the silent treatment. Well, piss on that anymore. I have to smile to myself, wondering what Tom would say if he knew I had such a thought.

We're old now. He's eighty, and I'm seventy-eight, and in the years I have left, I decided I was bloody well going to do as I please, that my old curmudgeon husband could like it or lump it. As my mother used to tell me, "You can't change another person, but you can change yourself."

At the end of the second week of my sleeping in the guest room, Tom announced that I was to return to our bedroom, "or else". The ultimatum reminded me of his announcement, a month before he retired, that whether I liked it or not, we were selling our house in Kingston and moving back to where we both grew up. It's something I had dreamed of doing, but Tom had always pooh-poohed the idea. I hadn't mentioned the possibility of moving home for years, so his announcement came like a gift from heaven. My only comment was, "Sounds good to me."

We've been back for twenty years now. Neither of us have any family left, except for our son who lives in Toronto, but we do have old friends, although by now, most of the ones left are in poor health.

When I left Tom's bed, I had no intention of not providing the good meals he's had all of our married lives, or not ironing the white shirts he wears, or not keeping the house clean. After moving into the guest room, my intentions were that I continue to look after him, after which, my time would be my own.

I said nothing when Tom nattered at me about having to sleep alone. My mind was made up. I was sleeping alone and that was that. Tom raved on about the foolishness of my spending money on a new mattress for the bed. I didn't tell him that I was planning to buy a new duvet and matching drapes. I'm shopping for a pattern of yellow roses.

How I love having that room to myself. If I am reading an especially good book, the minute I wake up, I hurry to have my morning pee, jump back into bed and read a half hour or so. Some mornings, I sneak downstairs, make myself a cup of tea and a piece of toast, hurry back upstairs to read for another hour.

On those days, Tom's surliness reaches a new high. When I finally arrive downstairs to begin cooking breakfast, I get the silent treatment. He sits at the table reading the morning paper, ignoring me, but I noticed he tucks into the plate of food I put in front of him. I want to say, "You're not helpless. Does it ever occur to you to take a turn at making the morning coffee and eggs?" Instead, I think about the book I'm reading, and how wonderful it is to have that comfortable bed to myself.

I think about other people and their beds. There was a time I assumed everyone had a bed somewhere. I know the homeless don't have beds. God knows there's enough in the newspapers about the scarcity of homes and beds for street people. When I visit our son in Toronto, and I see the homeless standing on the sidewalks begging or trying to sell their newspapers, I wonder what it must be like, not to climb into the same bed every night, not have a place to sleep, to make love, to burrow in, to have respite from the daily grind. I don't take the offered paper for sale, but I empty my change purse into the waiting hand.

I spend two weeks every Fall with our son, Jason. We take in a few plays, eat out a lot, and Jason drives me to visit some old friends who live there. I always have such a good time on my Toronto visits. Tom refuses to accompany me, and doesn't want to hear anything about my time in Toronto when I return home. It's just as well.

A few weeks after I moved from the marital bed, we were eating breakfast one day, Tom grumbling, and me not paying attention. He held his coffee mug out for a refill. "You haven't heard a word I've said."

"Want another piece of toast?" I asked him.

"No, I don't want another Goddamn piece of toast. I want an answer to my question. Are you, or are you not, moving back into that friggin' bed with me?"

It was strange to hear Tom talk like that. Even after he became badly crippled with arthritis, and had to deal with serious bowel problems, he never swore.

"That Goddamn laxative I took last night didn't work."

Here we go. The morning laxative report. I got up from the table and got the prunes from the refrigerator. "I keep telling you to eat some prunes every day."

He pushed the dish of prunes away. "You didn't answer me. I want to know. When are you moving back into our bed?"

"Not tonight, Josephine." I began the washing up.

He reached for his cane and got to his feet. "I'd like to thrash you with this," and he waved the cane at me.

"I just bet you would, Tom, but you know I'd be out that door for good, don't you?"

The image of him hitting me with his cane was comical. His six-foot-two, one-hundred-and-eighty-pound body towering over my skinny five-foot-two frame made me want to giggle. I turned back to the sink and the breakfast dishes. When he had left the room, I thought how easy it would be to stop the animosity between us. All I had to do was do what I was told, behave the way I had all during our marriage. *God, I'm getting as difficult as he is. I don't have to aggravate him with my smart-ass answers. The minute I finish here I'm going out for a walk. Clear my head.*

It was a June day, warm and sunny, and our yard man was working on the shrubs at the front of the house. I could see Tom standing in the living room window watching me. I nodded to Martin Crowe and kept moving. If I stopped to chat, I would return home to one of Tom's silly jealous tirades. Martin was fifty with a wife and house full of kids, but that didn't stop Tom from accusing me of flirting with him. I decided to walk down town to do a few errands. Years ago, when Tom and I returned to Cape Breton for a quieter life, I had hoped that he would become involved in some volunteer work. If anything, we had less of a social life than we had in Kingston.

I made friends at church, and in the volunteer groups I chose to join. Since my retirement, every time I left the house to attend a meeting, or meet a friend, I had to put up with what I called his Black Angus face. At first, I tried inviting people in, but he was so unfriendly to our guests, that I gave that up. There were only a few old friends he would spend time with.

I decided to do a few turns around a little down town park after I did my bank and post office errands. I enjoyed the beautiful garden tended by the local Horticultural Society, and usually sat on the bench near the roses for a few minutes.

When we were first married, and things were going well between Tom and me, he used to buy me roses on our anniversary. The first roses he gave me were gorgeous red roses. I thanked him profusely, told him I loved the roses, gave him a kiss, and whispered, "Next year buy me yellow roses. I like red, but I love yellow."

"What kind of a color is yellow for roses?" he asked me. The only rose worth looking at is red as far as I'm concerned."

So I got red roses for several anniversaries, then after five or six years, no roses at all.

Shortly before our eighth anniversary, our only child, Jason, was born. He was a healthy, beautiful baby. I was beside myself with joy.

Tom disapproved of my plans to stay home until Jason was old enough for school. He complained about the loss of my teaching income for those years. That was a weak argument. By that time, Tom was a senior school principal, making good money. I thought it had more to do with my having less time to cater to him, now that I had a baby to look after. I thought time would take care of his jealousy, that when Jason began walking and talking, Tom would begin to enjoy our darling boy. That never happened. Tom always had work excuses when I suggested that he spend time with Jason. I did what I could to make things different between the two of them, but Jason knew that his father didn't have the interest in him that he saw other fathers had in their sons.

When Jason was five, he began school, and I returned to my old grade two classroom in the school two blocks away from our house. Tom left the house before eight in the morning, giving Jason and me a half hour to tidy the kitchen, decide what we wanted for lunch, then set out for our walk to school.

Jason was an easy child. He loved school, took in everything with such eagerness. It bothered me that Tom didn't appreciate our son, and it bothered me that Jason, even as a child, was aware that his father never praised him. When he was in grade four and won first prize in the city Science Fair, he said, his voice full of sadness, "Mom, how come Dad never acts proud when I bring home a prize?"

Oh well, that's all water under the bridge now. Jason has a successful teaching career in Toronto, far away from his father's fault-finding. He writes me wonderful letters, letters Tom doesn't want to read. Every birthday Jason used to wire me yellow roses. My birthday is late September, and the roses arrived at my school. Now that I'm retired, he sends me a generous cheque with a card. I miss getting the roses, but I know, as well as Jason, that roses arriving at the house from him would set Tom off.

It was bad enough when one of Jason's letters arrived.

Tom seemed to take pleasure in asking, "Another letter from your queer son?"

Jason was twenty, and home from university for Christmas, when he told us he was gay. I'll never forget the look on Tom's face. He turned on me. "This is your doing, making him into a Mamma's boy. I warned you. I told you to stop spoiling him." Tom slammed out of the room, and I held my arms out to my son. I held him and we had a little cry together.

I feasted my eyes on the yellow roses for another minute, then got up and did two turns around the small park.

More than one friend, over the years, asked me why I stayed in the marriage. I thought about the women in fiction who had the guts to strike out on their own. I must have read *The Book of Eve* six times, when it first came out. I still remember what Eve took with her when she left her miserable husband; a copy *of Wuthering Heights, a* poetry anthology, and a small radio given to her by her son.

I could never leave the comfort of my home and live in a cold, musty, old basement apartment, manage on less than a hundred dollars a month. I like the things that are mine. My books, the Wedgewood china, the sterling silver, my collection of Mennonite quilts.

If I had to name the one thing Tom would miss if we had divorced and moved on, it would be his garden. Our yard used to be the neighbourhood show place. Tom was a gifted gardener, and gardening was his one extravagance. He grew everything but roses.

I used to have to drag him to the tailors to order a new suit. He was disinterested in clothes, so much so, that I would choose the ties to wear with the white shirts he insisted on wearing. It made me cross that he refused to wear coloured shirts. I also chose his socks and sweaters. One of the worst fights we ever had was over a worn out, twenty-year-old leather belt which he refused to replace. That Christmas I bought him the most expensive belt I could find, and threw the old one out in the trash. It was my throwing away the belt that caused such a row.

He hated spending money on clothes, but nothing was too costly for his garden. He had fifteen flower beds in our yard, and called them by name; the tulip garden, the geranium garden, the impatiens garden, the lily garden. He planted every exotic shrub known, and I lost count of the variety of perennials around the place. Having to give up gardening was an incredible disappointment to Tom.

Not a day goes by that I don't say a prayer of thanks for the years I taught school. I loved being a teacher. It got me out of the house, kept me close to Jason, gave me a life of my own, and provided me with wonderful friends and a good pension. When I worked, my salary went into the family pot, and Tom controlled that. The day my first pension cheque arrived, I announced to Tom that I was going to be in charge of how it was spent.

I thought he was going to have a heart attack. He sputtered, "Well, you'll damn well pay for half the groceries and utilities."

"Fine with me," was my answer.

Every month, when he passed me a piece of paper with the amount I owed written on it, I sat down and wrote him a cheque. How sweet it is to have the rest of my cheque to spend any way I please. I think, of all our unsolved issues, my handling my own money is the most painful for poor Tom.

The area in our marriage that gave us the least trouble was sex. Tom was good in bed. I enjoyed sex as much as he did. I used to tease him, *Tom, it's for the needy, not the greedy*.

When Jason was little and wanted to climb into bed with us, Tom refused to allow it. He said it wasn't healthy, but I knew the real reason was that Tom didn't like sharing time with me. Whenever I hear the words, *secret sorrow*, I think of that.

Long after getting an erection became a problem for Tom, he refused to talk about it. I think sex was the one part of our lives together that he felt O.K. about. I could go to bed full of anger at something he had done or said, and the way he reached out for me, the way he touched me would make me forget my anger.

On my walk home that day, I thought about the differences in my life and Tom's. Aside from a couple of old friends, he didn't see a soul, other than me, whereas I had many invitations to go here and there with friends. I couldn't accept them all. I spent several hours each week in volunteer work, but then I had the good health to do so, while Tom was confined because of his health. I knew he hated my leaving the house to go anywhere. One day, I told him he had no one but himself to blame for being lonely.

His answer was, "When a man has a wife, he isn't supposed to be lonely." He had such a sad look on his face when he said that. It reminded me of what had attracted me in the first place. It was his telling me about being raised without a mother. His mother died when he was two, and he and his father moved in with his fraternal grandparents.

Tom had no warm memories of love in that austere household. When he told me this, he added, "I liked being with you the minute I met you. You were so full of life. You made my lonely feelings evaporate."

I suppose it was his neediness that did me in. His neediness, and the knowledge that he was intelligent and ambitious. Memories of being depression kids made us both work hard for a home and security. Pity we had such different views on other matters. I grew up in a house full of laughter and making the best of things, whereas Tom's childhood was spent being quiet, having to listen constantly to the doom and gloom of his grandparents.

One day, long after we were married, when he was

going on about his childhood, I lashed out at him, "For God's sake, Tom, think of the wonderful life we have right now. Today. You're driving me crazy going on about the past."

It was almost noon when I left the park and headed for home. I planned turkey sandwiches and a salad for lunch. Tom would likely sit at the table and grumble about how long I had been gone.

He was sitting on the front verandah that day waiting for me. I expected to hear a litany of complaints, but he didn't say a word. When I started to walk by him, and into the house, he put a hand out and stopped me. "There's a surprise for you on the dining room table."

When I went inside, there it was, a bouquet of yellow roses.

Tom followed me inside, his eyes staring at me as I leaned over and smelled the roses. "They're beautiful, Tom."

How memory can force itself upon you. I remembered the day I asked for yellow roses so long ago. I stood there, my hands in the pockets of my denim skirt, silent, and my tears were silent.

"I phoned the florist and asked to have them delivered. They were here within the hour," he said.

I waited for him to say something else.

When he didn't speak, I asked him. "Am I forgetting something? What's the occasion?"

"No special occasion. I just thought you'd like them."

Tears ran down the sides of his nose. "I'm trying to apologize for the way I acted this morning."

I looked at my old-man husband. I didn't much like him.

I knew shortly after we were married that he was going to be a difficult man to live with. Back then divorce was unheard of, but even knowing all that, I can't say I'm sorry I stayed married to him. He gave me my wonderful son. When I was young, my mother advised me, "Make sure you marry a man who will be faithful, a man who will work hard." Well, Tom fulfilled both requirements. She forgot to add marry a man with a sense of humour, a man who loves children.

I took a tissue out of my pocket and wiped away his tears. I led the way to the kitchen. "Sorry I'm a bit late for lunch. We're having sandwiches. Come talk to me while I make them."

That night, after Tom was settled in bed, and I was in my nightgown, and had taken care of my nightly ritual of face cleansing, putting lotion on my legs and feet, checking that my book and a glass of water were on my bedside table, I went into Tom's room and climbed into bed.

When he reached out to turn the lamp on, I stopped him. I wanted to talk to him in the dark.

"Here's the deal," I told him. "I'll spend thirty or forty minutes here every night. Give you time to relax and get ready for sleep. Then I'm going back to the guest room and my book."

He let out a little sigh. It made me think of a child agreeing reluctantly to do as the mother said.

I moved close against his back, the way we had always slept together, my face at the nape of his neck, my toes reaching the backs of his legs. He reached his arm around to touch me. I patted him on the shoulder and said, "Go to sleep."

The half hour I spend nestled against Tom's back at bedtime, changed things between us. He stopped grumbling so much. He even took a turn once in a while doing the morning coffee and eggs. He remains a difficult man to live with, but sitting across from him at the breakfast table, I feel grateful for small mercies.

DOG FIGHT

Enid was planning to leave her husband. She had been thinking of leaving for years, truth be told. Years ago, she asked her mother, on her seventy-fifth birthday, "Ma, do you have any regrets about spending your whole life doing for others?" Her mother's terse reply was, "You bet I do. And I have regrets about not doing some things that I wanted to do."

It had taken some time for Enid to decide she was really going to leave George. Now the arrangements were made. *Can't back down now, old girl*, she told herself as she carried the pot of coffee and plate of toast to the table.

"I'll have a couple of eggs," George mumbled at her. "Sunny-side up."

"Make your own sunny-side ups, old man," she told him. She slathered strawberry jam on a piece of toast. "Might as well begin practice cooking for yourself. This time next month I'll be living in my senior's apartment, and you'll be on your own."

Enid, that's a thoughtless way to put it, she told herself. Suddenly, she felt mean, not frying George's eggs for him. She got the eggs out of the fridge for his breakfast. Her toast could keep. George would be fixing his own eggs soon enough.

George reached under the table and patted their cocker spaniel. He leaned down and murmured, "Let her go to her damn senior's place. We'll make out just fine, won't we, Buddy?"

"What do you mean "we"? I'm not moving without Buddy!"

George glared at her. "You're damn well not taking Buddy with you." His voice was full of indignation. "You can't take him anyway. They don't allow pets in those dinky units."

"They do in this building," Enid told him, a triumphant grin on her broad face. It had taken her months to find a place that allowed pets.

Enid had felt alone through most of their marriage. She might as well be alone in peace. She knew she would have to be the one who moved. George was attached to every inch of their small frame house, the house they bought right after they married.

There had been few changes made over the years. George even had a fit when she papered and painted. He hated change. He always wanted things to stay exactly the same, even his beloved garden. One time Enid brought home a peony bush to plant and he insisted she take it back. He said, "Those damn things bloom for a month and make an awful mess, and they bring ants into the house with them."

The locality of the house was important to George, only a fifteen-minute walk to the coffee shop where he and his old pit buddies met daily.

When she placed his eggs in front of him, George pushed them away and roared at her, "I'll roast in hell before I let you take Buddy with you!" At that moment their daughter Greta arrived. "You two at it again? I could hear you several doors away. What is it this time?"

George spoke first. "She says she's taking Buddy with her."

"Buddy's mine," Enid told her daughter. "And I've got the papers and receipts for his care to show it."

Greta was like her father when it came to change. She disapproved of her mother's plans to move to a place of her own. She couldn't understand why her mother was upsetting everyone. Besides being an inconvenience, it was an embarrassment. When Greta's husband died five years ago, and their only son moved out to get married, Greta religiously maintained the same routines she had all her married life. She gave her son's old room its weekly dusting, and both her son's closet, and her husband's closet were in the same tidy shape they had always been in.

"So it's Buddy, again, is it?" She sat down and helped herself to a piece of cold toast. "You two have been fighting over that dog since the day you got him twelve years ago."

Enid laughed. "You've got that right, and the rows we

had over Buddy were far more serious than the ones we had over money or politics. We fought over Buddy for days before I bought him. Then one day I just went to the kennels, bought Buddy, and brought him home."

"And Dad took a week or two to warm up to Buddy. Remember how he refused to allow Buddy to sleep in your bedroom? God, I remember that awful row." Greta's eyes were filled with disapproval. "Mom, that was when you changed the den into a bedroom for yourself."

"That was just an excuse to stop sleeping with me." George growled.

"I was relieved to get out of that damn double bed, your cold feet and the way you hogged all the covers," Enid snapped.

The next day Enid began packing in earnest. She wasn't taking much; the bed and the television she had bought for herself, some bedding, half the dishes, silver, pots, a few favourite pictures and ornaments.

Enid had always been careful with money and had a healthy savings account. With savings and her pension from her nursing job, she knew she could support herself. She was well able to take care of herself and Buddy.

George didn't have a clue about managing money. She thought, *George is going to be in for an awful shock when he begins running the house on his own.*

As she was wrapping dishes in newspaper, George walked into the kitchen. "What the hell do you think you're doing? Put those dishes back in the cupboard where they belong!"

"Don't start in, old man. Count your lucky stars that I'm not filing for a divorce. If I did that, you would have to buy my half share of the house, you know."

His face turned a mix of purple and red. She thought he was going to hit her. He sat down at the kitchen table and looked up at her. "You're making a damn fool of yourself, Enid. What are people going to say when they hear you're leaving me after all these years?"

"I'm not worried about what people are going to say, George." She continued to pack dishes.

"What will you do if I find a new woman?"

She stopped packing and gave him a baleful look. "George, you haven't had any air in your tire for years. How are you going to get a new woman?"

"Another woman might turn me on."

"Good luck, George," she said, and she meant it.

Buddy padded into the kitchen and settled at George's feet. Enid couldn't decide which of them had the saddest face.

She poured two cups of coffee and sat across the table from George. "Look, George, when I told you I wanted to live on my own, you said you couldn't understand why. I'm going to tell you again. You've never been interested in anything I was interested in. All the years we've been married, you never showed me any real affection. Sex was always, Wham-Bam-Thank-You-Ma'am. All you ever cared about was your damn job in the pit and your fishing cronies. All you and I have ever done is bicker and fight. I want the years I have left on this earth to be peaceful ones."

George picked Buddy up and held him close. "How am I going to get along without Buddy?"

Enid resumed her packing. Her heart had long been hardened against this man who could say "How am I going to get along without you?" to a dog and not to her. Besides, what was there to say to a man when you just didn't want to live with him anymore.

George stood up and waved a fist at her. Buddy slid to the floor and scampered out of the room. "You and your damn feelings, Enid. I'm sick to death of you and your damn feelings!"

"I know George. I know."

He knocked his chair over as he rushed out of the room.

When Buddy returned to the kitchen, Enid picked him up and gave him a hug. "Poor old George," she said to the dog. "He's upset now, but he's going to be alright. His life will be more peaceful, too."

She kissed the top of Buddy's head. "This move isn't going to be all peaches and cream for me either, Buddy. It was a hard decision for me to make at my age. When the dust settles, we'll invite George over for a meal. You'd like that, wouldn't you?" She put Buddy down and finished up her packing.

DON'T WAIT UP

Betty Arden, at thirty-four, was in love with Gus Foley. She wanted kind, gentle, Gus for a husband, and she wanted to have a baby. She felt in her heart that she and Gus were made for each other.

Betty was a primary teacher, and while she loved spending her days with seven-year-olds, she longed for a child of her own. In those days, in the thirties, married women were expected to give up their teaching career for hearth and home. Betty was ready to do just that. The fly in the ointment was Gus's mother.

Thirty-eight years old, Gus lived with his mother, the best cook and housekeeper in town. She lived to take care of Gus and she kept close track of his every move. She managed to scare away a few women who would have liked to have been Mrs. Gus Foley.

Gus knew that his mother would have one of her dramatic heart attacks when he told her he had made up his mind to marry Betty. He knew his mother would interfere, just as she had when he had dated other women. This time, he decided he wasn't going to stand for her manipulating. A couple of times he had thought he was in love, but this time it was different. This time he was in love for real. He was living for the day Betty would become his wife.

Everyone in town, except Gus's mother, whose name was Hannah, thought Betty and Gus made a lovely couple. They were both teachers. Betty taught in the Protestant primary school and Gus taught math in the Catholic high school.

Gus's Aunt Em's description of the pair: two peas in a pod. Both were short and a little on the plump side, Gus with pale blond curly hair and pale blue eyes, and in contrast, Betty's black hair, long and straight and her eyes a dark brown.

On the evening of the first day of the new school term, Gus headed for his Aunt Em's. He dropped in on Em for an hour or so the evenings he didn't have a date with Betty. This was a great source of dissatisfaction for Hannah. She didn't like Gus spending evenings away from home, and waited up for him no matter how often he objected.

One day, when Hannah was taking afternoon tea with Em, she referred to Betty as that "plump Protestant girl who lived in one of the row of miners' houses."

"Gus would be lucky to have Betty Arden for a wife," was Em's testy reply. "She's a wonderful young woman, and if I were you, I'd make the effort to be nice to her. She just might become your daughter-in-law."

That set Hannah off. "She's a Protestant for God's sake! But of course she'd turn Catholic in a minute if she thought she could marry into our family. Well, I won't have it. Em, if I find out you're encouraging my Gus to even consider that girl as a future wife, I'll skin you alive."

Em started to laugh. "I'd like to see you try. Look Hannah, Gus isn't getting any younger, and neither are you. Do you want to go to your grave knowing he'll be a fuddy-duddy old bachelor?"

Hannah reached up the sleeve of her blue silk paisley dress for her handkerchief, and started to dab at her eyes. "I can't bear the thought of his leaving me. He's all I've got to live for, Em."

"For God's sake Hannah, can't you see how happy Gus is whenever he's in the same room as Betty. Don't you want your son to be happy?"

Hannah pursed her lips. "He's perfectly happy unmarried and living at home."

"You've got to be the most selfish person on God's green earth, Hannah Foley."

"And you're a bad influence on my son!" Hannah slammed her teacup down on its saucer and rushed out of the house.

When Hannah complained to Gus about his frequent visits to Em, Gus reminded her with as much patience as he could muster, "For God's sake Ma, Em's your sister, a widow, with her only son living hundreds of miles away."

The visits to his Aunt Em were a rest from his mother's smothering. Not that he didn't appreciate and love his mother. After all, she had devoted her life to him, reminding him at least once a month that he had been a change-of-life baby, and after his father, who had been a doctor, died of a heart attack, twelve year old Gus was all she had to live for. Now that she was nearing eighty, Hannah reminded him often that it was his duty to take care of her.

Betty knew from her conversations with Em that Hannah was bound and determined that Gus remain single.

One day over a cup of tea, Betty told Em, "I can't do anything about his mother's objections to his getting married. I know Gus loves me, and we will get married, but Em, it's got to be soon. I'm tired of his putting off telling her. Gus said that he expected his mother to be upset, but that he didn't expect her to be rude to me. It embarrassed him. He didn't object too much when I told him I thought it would be a good idea if I saw as little as possible of his mother."

Em refilled their teacups. "The main problem is that Gus hates conflict. He's like his father, he'll do anything to avoid it. One of these days Hannah will go too far and he won't take it. Just the other evening I asked him when he was going to get up the gumption to tell his mother that he was going to get married. All he said was, "Soon.""

Betty said, "I suppose if he hadn't been giving into her for years, he wouldn't keep putting off telling her. There are a few situations where he stood up to her: his evenings out, the time he spends with me, and Hannah's nosing around his bedroom."

Em continued, "When he was sixteen, he told Hannah that from that day on he would clean his own room. What a racket there was over that. It went on for weeks. She finally gave in when he came home one day and showed her the lock he had bought for his bedroom door."

Gus told her, "I need my room to be my private place. I don't want anyone, even you, Ma, in my room. I'll keep it clean, and you are to stay out of it. If I find out you've been moving my stuff around, I'll go and stay with Aunt Em." Well, I guess she screamed bloody murder. She told him he could pack up and move in with me anytime he felt like it."

"The minute the words were out of her mouth, she collapsed in a heap on the floor." Em imitated Hannah. "Brandy, I need brandy. It's my heart." Believe me, Betty, Gus has seen the brandy scene often. He told me she never mentioned his room again. As far as he knows, his room is out of bounds to her. Her one request was that he didn't install the lock. She said she couldn't bear it if anyone found out he kept a lock on his bedroom door."

On a warm September evening, Gus and Em sat out on her back verandah enjoying a beer. The beer was another thing Gus counted on when he visited Em. His mother was death on drinking and would have a fit if she found out. Another thing he counted on was that Betty would often join them for a beer and a chat.

Betty lived four streets away from Em in the miner's house she had lived in all her life. Gus was only invited there when Betty was having friends in. He stayed on when the guests left. Those few hours were precious, the only time they had to be alone.

Gus passed a beer to Em. "Beats me Em, you eat like a starving teenager, drink a few pints of this stuff every day and stay so thin. You and Ma are the skinniest women in town."

"Never mind talking about how skinny I am. I want to

hear about the first day back to school. You look a bit tired."

"Well, the day was hectic." He changed the subject. "You know Betty spent the last week of the school holidays in Halifax visiting a friend. Well, I thought she'd be over-joyed to see me, but when I picked her up after school, she sure didn't act that way. In fact, she didn't even kiss me hello. You would have thought I was a taxi driver, not her boyfriend."

Em shook her head. "For a man with a degree, you sure act brainless sometimes. Did you ever stop to think that she might find herself another man?"

"Bite your tongue, Em. You know how I feel about Betty. I just wished Ma liked her. You'll be pleased to hear that I finally told Ma this morning I intend to marry Betty."

"God, I wish I could have seen the look on her face when you told her. Bet she looked like she was hit on the head with a shovel."

"She stomped upstairs, slammed her bedroom door shut hasn't said a word to me since."

"She expects you to wait until after her demise to marry, you know. Our parents both lived 'til their late nineties. Doesn't that worry you? And don't get me started on how that sister of mine treats Betty. If I were Betty I would have dropped you long ago. For God's sake, Gus, you two have been dating for over a year."

Gus glanced at his watch. "I thought for sure Betty would drop by for a visit with us this evening."

"Well, she isn't going to. She phoned me earlier to tell me she wouldn't be by this evening."

Gus felt morose. He looked at his watch again and

reached for his beer. "Maybe Ma will be in bed by now."

Em passed him the dish of peppermints. "Wishful thinking. Better chew a handful of these before you head home."

The following Sunday, Gus and Betty met for their usual Sunday lunch at Lawrey's restaurant, the best place in town to eat. It was also a quiet place on Sundays.

When their orders were taken and cups of steaming coffee served, Gus said, "Order something light. Ma's cooking a huge roast of beef for her dinner party this evening."

When Betty looked surprised, Gus asked, "Ma phoned and invited you, didn't she?" Betty remained silent.

Gus covered his face with his hands. His voice was full of embarrassment when he spoke. "We're going to her damn dinner party together or we're not going at all." He reached across the table and touched the engagement ring on Betty's left hand. "Do you know what I thought? I thought that this would be a good time to announce our engagement."

"Gus, You know I hate going to your place. We've been going out for over a year, and I can count the number of occasions I've been to your home on the fingers of one hand."

Gus reached across the table and used the pads of his thumbs to wipe away the gathering tears. "Betty, you've been so good about putting up with her."

"I put up with her because I love you, and because I know you love me and that you aren't taken in by her manipulating."

"You've told her we're engaged. I thought she would at least have me over for tea." Betty continued, "I'll never forget the day you took me home to meet your mother.

Remember how intimidated I had been by the size of your old Victorian house, the beautiful furniture, the heavy damask drapes, the paintings on the wall."

"I can still see your mother walking toward me in her black taffeta dress and three strands of pearls, looking like a thin version of the Queen Mother. I felt awkward when your mother held out a bony hand and said, "Welcome to my home, Miss Arden.""

I managed to say, "It's a beautiful home, Mrs. Foley,"

"Then she said, "It will be Gus's home when I'm gone. I can't tell you the number of girls in this town who are anxious to share this beautiful house with Gus.""

Then she turned to you and said, "I've invited Em and two other ladies to join us. I decided that if I was going to cook a company dinner, I might as well ask a few of my lady friends."

I remember how embarrassed you looked. Your face turned beet red. I also remember feeling relieved to see that one of the ladies was your Aunt Em. The other two were members of your mother's church guild. It was the most nerve-wracking meal I've ever eaten. The food was delicious, roast beef with all the trimmings and a superb lemon pie. It was handling the Limoges china and sterling silver cutlery that made me anxious, along with the stream of questions directed at me by your Mother."

"I remember that day well," Gus said, making a sad face. "I remember Em snapping at Ma, "Betty isn't applying for a job, Hannah. And you could call her by her first name. I'm sure you know it.""

"I also remember feeling more nervous by the minute,

blurting out "Ma makes the best lemon pie in town."

"That was when your mother said to me, "I understand you live alone since your parents died. You probably don't have much need to cook." You jumped in after Em gave you a poke in the ribs with an elbow. "Betty cooks and entertains beautifully. She has wonderful get-togethers for her friends and everyone raves about her cooking"

Gus said, "Let's enjoy our roast beef sandwiches. I get a pain in my gut every time I remember the way Ma treated you that evening." He took a bite of his sandwich. The evening had gone downhill after he had stuck up for Betty. His mother monopolized the conversation, talking to her two church friends about a church bazaar. It was as if Betty weren't there. When Ma asked Em if she were going to make her famous oatcakes for the bake table, Em didn't answer her.

Instead, she folded her napkin neatly, placed it beside her dessert plate. She said, "I'm afraid I have to take my leave. I have some friends dropping by for a visit this evening." You pushed your chair back from the table and told Em, "I'll walk you home."

"I remember," Gus said. I told Ma, "You and the ladies can continue to work on the bazaar plans in peace. I'm sure you won't miss us."

Gus put his sandwich down. "I wish that evening had never happened. Ma and I had an awful row the next day. When I told Em about the fight she told me that she was glad I wasn't letting Ma get away with slighting you. She also said there were too many instances when I reminded her of my father who wanted peace at any price."

After that first meeting with Hannah, Betty accepted

few invitations to Gus's home. She suggested to Gus that they take Hannah out for dinner once a month. Em also came along. The restaurant was public territory so it was difficult for Hannah to make a scene there.

Gus thought it was generous of Betty to see his mother at all. He didn't expect that Betty would ever enjoy his mother's company.

Gus knew his mother was a royal pain in the ass. The thing was, she was his mother and he couldn't do anything about that. He appreciated Betty's patience with the situation.

The Sunday Betty told Gus she hadn't received an invitation to Hannah's dinner party, her patience had flown the coop. "I'm not going," she said quietly.

"I don't expect you to go, Love. We'll take a drive into Sydney, have dinner at the Royale."

Betty's smile thanked him for not trying to coax her into going. "How about asking Em to join us? She loves the food at the Royale."

Gus nodded. "She won't want to go to Ma's anyway if we're not going to be there."

When they dropped by Em's to tell her the evening plans they found out the reason for Hannah's dinner party.

"I just found out today that your mother's having that dinner to introduce a girl to you. Someone who is in town visiting her aunt. The aunt is a friend of Hannah's."

Gus said, "I suppose she's a lovely Catholic girl, and comes from a well-off family."

Betty began to laugh.

"What's so funny?" Gus asked.

Em spoke. "The situation is funny. There's my dear sister doing anything she can to keep you from getting married. If I know her, the plan is to find someone to take you away from Betty."

Gus's face turned glum. "Guess that's why Betty didn't get invited to dinner tonight."

Em said. "Gus, your mother is not a nice person. Well the three of us aren't going to her damn dinner party. Let her stew waiting for us. Let's go. Are we eating at my favourite place?"

The next day Hannah stormed into Em's kitchen when Em was washing her breakfast dishes. "You were behind Gus not making an appearance last evening, weren't you?"

"Don't know what you're talking about, Sis." Then she flicked a dishtowel at Hannah. "Keep up interfering with your son's life he's going to leave home before he's married, not when he's married."

Hannah lowered herself into a kitchen chair and started to cry. "I don't want to lose him, Em." She took the box of tissue Em offered. "You know he promised me he would never leave me."

"Sweet Jesus, Hannah, that was when he was twelve years old, the year his father died."

Hannah's mouth was pinched. "Well, I don't want him to marry that old maid school teacher he's going out with. He can do better than that. She isn't good enough for him."

"You're like a dog with a bone, Hannah. You always have to have it your way. Keep it up, woman, and you'll see little of your son after he's married."

"I'll thank you not to speak to me in that tone of voice." She threw the box of tissue at Em and flounced out the kitchen door.

A week after that morning in Em's kitchen, Hannah had another dinner party planned. This time Betty got an invitation. It was Hannah's eightieth birthday and she decided to throw a party for herself.

Em dropped by Hannah's the Sunday afternoon before the birthday party. She was hoping to meet the girl Hannah had picked out for Gus.

Hannah greeted her, all smiles." There's someone here I want you to meet. Join us for tea."

"Hannah's about as transparent as clear cellophane," Em reported to Betty the next day.

When Betty asked her, "What's her name? What was your impression of her?"

"Her name is Angela Brown, and she's as smooth as silk, has an ingratiating smile, curly red hair, looked like she just stepped out of a fashion magazine. Definitely not Gus's type." She paused for a moment. "My God, Betty, you're not worried about Hannah and her foolishness, are you?"

Betty shook her head. "Of course not, Em. I'm as sure of Gus as if we were already married. But it does worry me that Hannah is going to such lengths to interfere in Gus's life."

A few days before Hannah's birthday party, Gus was sitting at his aunt's kitchen table, the expression on his face changing with each sip of beer. One minute his face was full of determination, the next confusion, the next anger.

"Aunt Em, I found out yesterday that Ma showed Angela Brown around my bedroom."

"Why the hell would she do that? And how did you find

out?"

"She was showing Angela my collection of academic awards. And I found that out because I ran into Angela in town and she gushed on and on about my framed certificates on the walls of my room."

"And did you have it out with your mother?"

"No, I didn't, Em. That would be an exercise in futility. But I did make a decision, and if Betty agrees with me, Ma will be in for a big surprise at her birthday party."

Sunday, the evening of the birthday party, there were twelve people around the huge dining room table enjoying the rack of lamb and bowls of vegetables prepared by Hannah. Besides Gus and Betty, Em and Hannah, there was Angela and her aunt, the Parish priest, and five of Hannah's close friends.

After Em and Gus cleared away the dinner plates, they returned to the dining room, one bearing a huge chocolate birthday cake, the other a tub of vanilla ice cream. Everyone sang Happy Birthday to Hannah.

Hannah stood to make her thank you speech. She began, "This is the best birthday party I've ever given!"

While the guests were applauding, Gus stood up, reached for Betty's hand and pulled her up beside him. "I have wonderful news, Ma." He announced. He and Betty walked to the head of the table where Hannah stood, looking puzzled.

Betty told Em afterwards, "My heart was beating so hard, I couldn't trust myself to look at Hannah."

Gus put his hands on his mother's shoulders and said gently, "Sit down, Ma. He wanted her seated before he broke the news. He coughed to clear his throat. "Ma, Aunt

Em, Father Joe, and friends, Betty and I have an announcement to make. We got married in Sydney yesterday. Folks, meet my lovely bride."

Hannah began her hysterics. "How could you do this to me? You've spoiled my birthday party! Oh, you're a cruel, cruel son." Then she slid slowly to the floor.

Em was at her side in a moment holding out a flask of brandy. She winked at Gus. "I thought something like this was up, so I came prepared."

Half of the guests crowded around Betty and Gus, shaking hands and hugging. The other half tried to comfort Hannah.

Hannah remained sitting on the floor sobbing. She grabbed at Em. "Em, tell those two to get out of my house. I never want to see either of them again."

"They'll be gone in a few minutes, Hannah. Gus is collecting his packed suitcase. They're going on their weekend honeymoon. They have to be in school on Monday."

Em pulled her sister to her feet. "Get yourself together woman. You've got guests at your table, birthday cake to be served. The ice cream is beginning to melt."

Hannah stood tall. Her thin smile was grim and full of her suffering. "You can take care of my guests, Em." She added, "Before you do that, please help me into my bedroom. I must lie down."

Em and Hannah stood at the foot of the stairs as Gus descended, carrying a suitcase. He was grinning at Betty who was waiting at the front door. He paused at the bottom step and looked directly at his mother. "Ma, I hope you'll find it in your heart to be happy for us." Giving his mother and Em each a kiss, he hurried to join his wife.

THE GRAVEYARD DAY

Kate used to treasure the first hour of the day, that one precious hour before Don's ten-year-old daughter, Vanessa, woke up.

When Kate married Don, she had assumed that Nessa would eventually accept her. Kate had always been good with kids. Now, after three years of trying to form some kind of an alliance with her stepdaughter, she was ready to throw in the towel.

Don and Kate spent that early hour over coffee and breakfast, planning the day, discussing his Business Depot and her Children's Book Store. Kate made a point of never mentioning Nessa during that hour. She found out early in the marriage that if she began to discuss something con-

127

cerning Nessa, Don immediately became edgy.

More than once Don mentioned that he was pleased that they were both morning people, that he enjoyed their first hour of the day together. He often complimented Kate's efficiency in running the house. He had hated being a widower, had hired a series of housekeepers to do the cleaning and cooking. Unfortunately not one of them lasted more than a month.

Kate didn't have good memories of her first marriage. That marriage had been a disaster.

Don was opposite of everything her first husband had been. Don was a take-charge kind of man, owned a successful business, had loads of friends and was a loving father to Nessa. Kate wasn't aware of the constant indulgence until after they were married.

At the beginning of the marriage, Kate assumed Don accepted her just the way she was. A few months into the marriage, she was dumfounded when she realized that he expected her to conform to his idea of a wife and stepmother. When she did something that didn't please him, particularly something concerning Nessa, Kate felt as if she were walking on eggs.

Kate's place at the breakfast table faced the hallway, and every morning, as Nessa walked down the hall toward the kitchen, she would give Kate a cold, snotty look. Then, when she entered the kitchen and ran towards her dad, her face was all smiles. The routine was, kiss daddy good morning, ignore the wicked stepmother. Every morning Don would prod, "Sugar, say good morning to Kate." He had stopped urging Nessa to call her mom. He gave that up the day that Nessa, her eyes full of tears, had begged, "Daddy, please don't ask me to do that."

At first Kate had found it touching that Nessa talked about her mother constantly. She mentioned it to Don one day, and she was astonished at how upset he became.

"What else would expect? That's a natural thing for Nessa to do. It's important that she remember her mother. Talking about Mona helps her to do that."

"Of course it's important for her to remember her mother," Kate said. "I wasn't being critical, and I want both of you to know that I have no aspirations to take Mona's place."

Kate decided on a different tack. She began to encourage Nessa to talk about her mother. One day she said to Nessa, "Tell me about how your mother used to take you shopping."

Nessa looked at her with disdain and said, "I don't want to tell you anything about my mother. I only like talking about her with daddy." Kate didn't repeat that conversation to Don. She knew by then that if she did, they would end up arguing about Nessa's intent. Nor did she repeat to him the conversation she overheard between Nessa and a girlfriend. Kate was in the kitchen clearing away the lunch things and the girls were outside the kitchen window getting on their bikes.

Nessa's friend said, "You're stepmother is nice."

Nessa replied, "She's not my stepmother."

"Then what is she?"

"She's not anything."

"But she lives here in your house with your dad."

"Just because she lives here, it isn't her house. This is my house. I know where all Mommy's things are stored. I know all the special and secret things about this house, and I'm never going to share this house with her, no matter how smarmy nice she pretends to be. She'll leave us just like all the housekeepers did."

Kate's first inclination was to rush outside and tell Nessa she was a rude, spoiled brat. Instead she stood there, wiping the same spot on the counter over and over, tears of frustration mingling with the soap and water.

The graveyard day happened on a Sunday. It began with a morning ritual Kate had started as a way for the three of them to spend time together. She made a pot of coffee, filled a tray with bagels, croissants, cream cheese, and Don's favourite raspberry jam. She carried the tray into their bedroom along with the Sunday papers, and invited Nessa to join them. With pillows piled behind their backs, the tray stationed in the middle of the king-sized bed, they read and munched together.

On that particular Sunday, Kate had to cut short her time with them. She had promised to go to a furniture auction with her best friend, Jan.

Don was cool toward Jan. It hurt Kate that the two most important people in the world to her didn't care for each other. Don made a face when Kate reminded him about the auction, and told him she wouldn't be home for lunch.

"Can't you just go to the auction with her and come home for lunch?" Don asked.

Kate leaned over and kissed his handsome nose. "Darling, we agreed that we would have time for old friends."

Nessa was taking dainty bites from a croissant, her eyes glued to Don's face.

Kate asked her, "Nessa, would it be alright with you if your dad and I had a few minutes alone?"

Don put his coffee mug down on the tray. "Damn it, Katie. You're doing it again. Making Vanessa feel she's in the way."

Nessa's eyes filled with tears. "It's O.K. Daddy. I have to get dressed anyway. Remember the plans we made when you tucked me into bed last night? You said since Kate would be busy you would take me to visit Mommy's grave today."

Kate moved away from the bed quietly, grabbed the sweater and jeans she planned to wear, and headed for the shower. She had a sudden fantasy of Mona`s ghost hovering over the bed warning Don. "Better watch it, Don, there's a limit to what that woman will put up with."

Don followed her into the bathroom, closing the door. "Are we going to get the silent treatment again?"

Kate hated it when he used the pronoun, "we".

"Better the silent treatment than speaking my mind. God forbid that I should ever say how I really feel."

"You don't feel free to express your feelings?"

Kate busied herself creaming her face and didn't answer. She didn't have the heart, or the time for one of their Nessa discussions.

He said, "Katie, I'm getting sick and tired of this withholding act of yours."

Nessa opened the bathroom door, her face all puckered up. "Daddy are you and Kate fighting again?"

"Yes, we are, Nessa," Kate said quietly. "Married people often fight, and they usually do it in private."

"God damn it, Kate !" Don yelled. "Don't use sarcasm

on my daughter!"

The visit with Jan that Kate had so looked forward to wasn't fun, mostly because she was so full of sadness. After a couple of hours, Jan decided she wasn't going to find the table she was looking for, so they headed for their favourite restaurant and an early lunch.

"You're picking at your food, Kate." Jan said, "You only do that when you're upset about something."

"Same old stuff, Jan. God, you must be sick of my going on and on about Vanessa, the blue-eyed monster." Jan signalled the waitress. "Let's have some dessert. The chocolate cake here is fabulous." She reached across the table and gave Kate a reassuring pat. "Think of the times you've listened to my problems."

"It's beyond the problem stage. Kate held up a thumb and forefinger. "I'm this close to giving up. Oh, Jan, why didn't I listen to you when you urged me not to get married until I knew him better." Kate choked back tears. "I remember laughing when you told me that my brains had fallen between my legs, that I should just have a glorious affair with Don."

"Well, you did want to move in with Don and see how things worked out before getting married, but he refused that set-up because of Vanessa."

"Vanessa. She was in rare form this morning," Kate said, "but before I tell you about that, let me tell you what she did with the beautiful book I gave her for her birthday two weeks ago."

Jan rolled her eyes. "Let me guess. She lost it?"

"Worse than that. She destroyed several pages of it. A few days before her birthday, I told her I would like to make a party for her, but she turned down the offer with, "Daddy always takes me and my friends to a restaurant for my birthday. I want my birthday to be the same as always."

Kate took a bite of the chocolate cake. "I made a smashing birthday cake and invited them back to the house for cake and ice-cream. I could tell that Nessa agreed only because it was evident that Don wanted her to. He was there when she refused my offer of a party and I think, for once, he was embarrassed by the way she spoke to me."

"What happened about the book?"

"I gave her Robert Voura's "Such is the Nature of Horses." The illustrations in the book are absolutely gorgeous. Knowing how much she loves horses, I thought she would be thrilled with it."

"And?"

"When I was straightening up the family room that evening after Vanessa had gone to bed, I found the torn pages in the waste paper basket. The front page I had written a message on, and ten more pages. I'm sure she meant for me to find them."

"My God, what did you do?"

"I felt sick to my stomach, and so angry, I rushed up to her bedroom with the waste paper basket and the torn pages. She just looked at me with those old eyes of hers and shrugged." "Whoever did that must be very jealous of me."

"I told her I didn't believe that for a minute, that I knew that she deliberately ruined the book to hurt me. At that point Don came into the room. Jan, he was furious with me. He wanted to know how I could even think that Vanessa would do such a destructive thing."

"What did you say to him?"

"I was sarcastic. I said, "Right. I confess. I tore up ten pages of a sixty-five dollar book, thinking you would believe that your darling daughter did it, and that you would ship her off to the nearest boarding school.""

"What did he say?"

"He didn't say a word, and he barely spoke to me the next few days. Nessa loved every minute of it. She didn't let him out of her sight, cuddling up to him, giving him little sympathy pats."

"I take it you and Don eventually made up."

"Yeah, and you don't have to guess how," Kate said sadly. "A few nights after Nessa's birthday, he was in the mood for sex. After we made love, he asked me to just put the horse book episode behind us."

Jan's face was full of disbelief. "Is that it? No consequences for destroying a beautiful book? Does Don think because you own a bookstore that you can afford to have an expensive book mutilated?"

"I know. It sounds sick, doesn't it? I'm at my wits' end, Jan. I can't stand having that kid running my life. I've been day dreaming about looking for an apartment and telling Don that I was moving out until he was willing for us to get some family counselling."

Jan reached across the table for one of her hands. "You have to take care of yourself, Kate. You haven't been yourself for months."

"You know the worst part for me? That if this marriage is over, I'm going to have to go through another divorce." She started crying into her napkin. "I feel like a total flop when it comes to being a wife."

Jan squeezed her hand. "Change that to you're a flop

when it comes to choosing a husband."

Don and Vanessa weren't home when Kate returned that afternoon. There was a note from Don on the kitchen table. "Vanessa's grandmother called and invited us to come over when we returned from the graveyard. Too bad you weren't here to join us."

Mona's mother hadn't welcomed Kate into the family with open arms at first. She had been very reserved, but later on, when she got to know Kate, it was evident that she had come to like and respect her. Kate sensed Vanessa's grandmother was concerned about the way things were going. She shared Kate's concerns. Kate never repeated their conversations about Vanessa to Don.

Kate put the note down and said out loud, "To hell with it!" She made herself a bloody Mary, took a long relaxing bath, pulled on her terry robe, and put on a Billie Holiday tape. The peace was lovely.

It was good to have the time alone, not to have to monitor her words or actions. There were times in her marriage that she felt she was auditioning. "*I don't think you're going to get the part,*" she sometimes told herself.

She was sleeping soundly when Don came into the bedroom. She awoke to the sounds of his hanging his clothes in the closet. He pointed to the inch of bloody Mary left in the glass. "How many of those have you had?"

Kate sat up and stretched. "As a matter of fact, I didn't finish my first. You and Nessa have a nice day?"

"It would have been nicer had you been with us." He leaned over and opened the front of her robe. "Anything on under that?"

She pushed him away. He scowled. "I missed you today,

Kate. You know how much I hate it when you make Sunday plans that exclude Vanessa and me."

"We've been over this before Don. I know you don't agree with me, but I still think it would be better for Nessa if she spent some weekend time with her friends instead of being with us every minute."

He sat on the bed and began to massage her feet. "Vanessa still misses Mona so much. I wish you could have seen her little face at the graveyard today when she was putting flowers on Mona's grave. She said the saddest thing to me. She said, "Daddy, promise me that when I die, I'll be buried right here between you and Mommy."

Kate felt a sense of awe that a ten-year-old could wield that kind of power.

Don continued, "She told me that the time she misses Mona the most is on Sunday mornings when the three of us used to climb into bed together and read."

"Sunday mornings," she murmured. "You told me Mona hated mornings, that she hardly ever spoke until noon. You told me you and Mona had slept in twin beds." Kate knew she was babbling but she couldn't stop. "Don't you think that graveyard scene was a tad manipulative?"

He pushed her feet away. "She's only a child, for God's sake! Sometimes, Katie, you act very uncaring about Vanessa. She thinks you don't like her, that you're always planning things that don't include her."

Kate got up and rummaged for a blanket in the closet. In the doorway she turned to him. "Your denial is driving me nuts, Don. We need some professional help, and we had better get it soon."

He followed her down the hall and into the family room.

Kate had never seen him so angry. "I will not have you or anyone else meddling with my daughter's emotions."

"O.K., Don, maybe you and Vanessa don't need help, but I sure as hell do, and I know it. Don't you care that I feel I need professional help?"

Vanessa called from her bedroom. "I can't get to sleep, Daddy. I need you to come and sit with me."

Don turned away from her. "We'll continue this discussion in the morning."

Kate put a hand on his arm. "Don, it's not good for a child to have the kind of power Nessa has in this house. I'm asking you one more time. Please, let's get some family counselling."

"I discussed the idea of counselling with Nessa, and it upset her terribly." He turned and left the room.

Kate thought about her first marriage. It ended when she admitted that Robert had problems that had nothing to do with her.

She wanted to be able to understand what happened to her dreams for this second marriage. She thought she knew Don. Do we ever know anyone? At that moment she was feeling hurt and confused. She knew in her heart's deep core that she couldn't have a ten-year-old ruin her marriage, or live with a man who let that happen.

Kate knew that the Sunday brunches were over. The other thing she did know was that it was up to her to take charge of her life.

AGGIE'S
HAUNTED QUILT

eather MacDonald lost track of the number of stray cats her mother had housed and fed since her father died. Stray cats were Aggie's passion. Heather and her father had been allergic to cats, so at one time, Aggie had to content herself with one cat, and had to keep that one confined to the back porch.

Ten years ago, less than a month after Archie died, Aggie turned the house into a stray cat sanctuary. Heather imagined her mother, standing in the backyard in the dark of night, thumbing her nose to the sky and muttering, "I hope wherever you are, Arch, you know that I now have all the cats I want."

In the years since Arch's death, Aggie had become crippled with arthritis. She was also diabetic and deaf. Heather was trying to convince her mother to sell the house and move into a seniors' community. Every time Heather brought up the subject, Aggie would sing, *It's a Long Way to Tipperary* at the top of her lungs.

Aggie gave her cats more love than she ever gave her only child. As long as she could remember, Heather always seemed to irritate the hell out of her mother. Aggie's continual complaint was that she had been born a girl. Even now, with Heather in her fifties, Aggie still made wistful remarks about not having a son.

When Heather was a child, her mother reminded her of her preference for boys constantly. Fortunately, never a week went by that her father didn't tell Heather how much he loved her, how proud he was of her. She was grateful that her father had lived to see her graduate from college, marry Earl, and give birth to their darling twin daughters.

The time had come that Heather had been dreading for the last few years. Aggie, a month away from eighty, was getting harder to deal with by the day. She began quarreling with her cleaning woman, Alice, who had worked for the family for years. Some days Alice would be locked out, and the big old house Aggie used to take such pride in, began to look run down and neglected.

Aggie's appearance was another matter. While she had dressed in jeans and men's shirts for years, they at least were clean and ironed. Now the clothes Aggie wore were wrinkled and spotted with dabs of food. Then there was the smell of the place. Heather was now smelling cat pee when she reached the back door.

Heather had to make Aggie see that it was time for her

to move. The September day she set out to do so, Earl gave her a hug, and said, "Lots of luck, Sweetheart."

When Aggie opened the door, Heather passed her a beef casserole, still warm in a padded bag. Aggie lifted the Pyrex dish out of the bag and reached into the cupboard for a plate. No "Thank you", but then there never was.

"Would have been nice to sit and eat with some company like most people do," she grumbled.

"Mom, you eat supper with us every Monday, Wednesday, Friday and Sunday. Earl and I have to have some time to ourselves."

Heather hadn't quite figured out how Aggie had manipulated her into feeling responsible for supplying her meals. It started right after her father's death. Aggie just stopped cooking. She stopped shopping for groceries. It was worrisome for Heather to see the empty shelves, the piece of hard cheese keeping company with mushy old tomatoes and a carton of sour milk in her mother's refrigerator.

At first Heather enlisted the help of Meals on Wheels. Aggie left the meals they brought untouched. Before she knew it, Heather was either delivering her mother a nutritious meal, or inviting her to join her and Earl for supper. Earl claimed that anyone as plump as Aggie, had to be eating on the sly.

Aggie stood at the kitchen counter, wolfing down the beef casserole. One forkful for her and one forkful aimed at the cats clamouring at her ankles.

Heather usually left at this point. Besides being upset about what her mother was doing with the food she so carefully prepared, she, like her father before her, was allergic to cats.

Aggie spoke with her mouth full. "No meeting to run off to? No complaints about your blasted allergies?"

"Actually," Heather said, "I came over to talk to you about selling this big old house and moving into a seniors' unit. This is a perfect time of year to move."

Aggie slammed the half-eaten beef casserole on the floor. The cats tumbled over each other getting to it. Her eyes narrowed, her face turning an angry red. "You and Earl would like that wouldn't you? Put me away so you wouldn't have to do anything for me. And who would look after my cats? You're one pair of selfish pigs, you two".

Heather was prepared to find good homes for Aggie's cats. She knew there were five permanent residents but was never sure of how many transients were in the house at any given time. She didn't want to discuss the fate of the cats that day. Her intention was to plant the idea of selling the house. She glanced at her watch. "I promised Earl I'd take over at the Drug Store for a few hours. I'll come over this evening and talk some more about this. You've been complaining about looking after this place for a long time now. How hard it is finding someone dependable to do the mowing in the summer and the shoveling in the winter, all that stuff." Heather headed for the back door, Aggie at her heels.

"I know. I know alright. You're just like your father. Bossy. Think you know what's good for me." She was yelling. "Your father was a friggin' control-freak. Thought he knew everything, and you're just like him." Her voice lowered. "If I had a son, I'd be looked after properly."

Halfway to the Sydney Mall, Heather pulled the car over and parked for a few minutes. Her eyes were full of tears. She had heard the son lament hundreds of times, but it still hurt.

She had a hard time with the way Aggie talked about Arch. Aggie's foul mouth was the most hurtful change of all. Aggie had always adored Arch. She had clung to his every word, asked his advice about everything from how much salt to put in the stew to what to wear to a party.

Heather had memories of them going to a lot of parties. Arch owned the only drug store in town and he believed it was important for them to socialize. Heather conjured up the memory of the two of them heading out for one of their Saturday night house parties, Arch wearing a navy blue blazer and grey slacks, Aggie wearing her favourite red dress, with its long full sleeves and full skirt.

Heather remembered standing in the doorway with Alice. Alice was in her teens then, and Heather's baby-sitter. Heather remembered the ache in her little six-year-old-heart, as she watched them walk down the drive. The look on Aggie's face, gazing up adoringly at Arch, made Heather wish that her mother looked at her like that once in a while.

The next day was Saturday and Heather drove the few blocks to her mother's house with a dish of macaroni and cheese, Aggie's favourite meal. She planned to lay the groundwork for a serious talk the following day when Aggie would be joining her and Earl for the weekly after-church roast-beef dinner.

Aggie had given up attending church a year or so after Arch died, and began bad-mouthing the church and the minister so much that Heather and Earl avoided the topic of church. There began to be many topics to avoid. Aggie never wanted to talk about anything but her cats.

Alice's old Ford was in the driveway when Heather

arrived. She thought, *Poor Alice, how does she stand hours of that pee smell?*

She found Aggie and Alice in the dining room, arranging stacks of sheets on the dining room table. Aggie didn't look up from the pile of sheets she was counting. "What did you bring me today?"

"Macaroni and cheese." Heather was searching Alice's face for some clue as to what was going on. Alice moved directly behind Aggie and shrugged her bony shoulders at Heather. Her face said, *Don't ask me anything, because I don't know.*

Aggie grabbed the dish out of Heather's hands, rushed into the kitchen and shoved it in the oven. "This will do Alice and me for our noon meal. Don't plan on hanging around, we've got too much to do to bother with company."

Heather followed her into the kitchen. "What have you got to do?"

"Something that should make you and that skinny husband of yours very happy." Aggie went back to the dining room table. She held up her favourite patchwork quilt to Alice. "This goes in the pile of stuff that I'm taking to the old folks home."

Aggie was touching the feather stitching around the quilt patches with little reverent strokes. "Remember, Alice, when I found this old quilt at a yard sale? It was the day after the sweetest cat in the whole world was left on my doorstep. Remember?"

Alice nodded. "I remember, Aggie. That's why you named her Feather, after the stitches in the quilt."

Heather was remembering the endless yard sales her mother dragged her to over the years. Aggie had an eye for items for re-sale. She would wear down the owner, get items for a ridiculous amount, and then add them to her stock of gems for her weekly neighbourhood yard sale. Money made at the yard sales went toward the cost of cat care.

When Heather tried to explain to her husband how embarrassed she was by the card tables full of discarded stuff on her mother's lawn every Wednesday, he cautioned her, "Don't discourage her. It keeps her out of your hair for a few hours."

"But Dad left her plenty money. She doesn't have to do that."

He just hugged her and said, "I know Hon, I know."

Aggie poked her with a roll of drawer liner. "You can drive me around to look at those old people's places this afternoon and I'll choose one. But I'm not selling my house. I'm going to have Alice and her daughter move in here and run the place for me. You're right about it being too much for me, It's getting to be a real pain in the arse."

Heather stared at her mother. She had never heard her mother use the word arse in her life. Heather stared at Alice again. Alice shrugged her shoulders. "This is all news to me, Heather. First time your mother mentioned moving to me. I thought I was here to help her clean out closets."

Aggie spoke. "I decided to tell you both at the same time. No use chewing my cabbage twice."

"Mom, you have to sell the house. Having Alice move in, even if she wanted to do such a thing, just wouldn't work."

Alice moved behind Aggie and put a finger to her lips. Her face said, *You and I will talk later*.

Heather told her mother she'd pick her up around two and hurried out of the house.

Two weeks later Aggie moved into a seniors' apartment building situated on River Road. Aggie, in a rare good mood, said she thought the place was charming. She especially liked the view of the river. She said she chose that particular building because of their policy of allowing the residents to have a pet.

Aggie decided that Feather, her all-time favourite cat would accompany her to the apartment. She said she couldn't live without Feather and their nightly ritual. When Aggie was settled for sleep, Feather would jump on the bed, walk up and down on the patchwork quilt, knead Aggie's back for a few minutes. Then Aggie would turn down the quilt and Feather would snuggle into the crook of her arm and go to sleep.

Heather was taking Alice's advice and saying little about Aggie's grand scheme to have Alice look after the house and the cats. She agreed to just concentrate on getting her mother moved. Heather was more than willing to take Alice's advice. Alice was the best friend Heather had. She knew she could never have coped with Aggie over the years if it weren't for Alice.

When Arch died of a heart attack, it was Alice who took over and made the funeral arrangements. It was also Alice who acted as a buffer when Arch's will was read and Aggie learned that the Drug Store had been left to Heather and Earl.

The day of the big move, Heather said to Aggie, "Mom, I won't be running here every day with food, but I will pick you up on the regular days you come to our place for your evening meal."

Aggie waved her pudgy hands at her. "Feather and I are going to be just fine. There's a convenience store around the corner."

That night, Heather and Alice shared a pot of tea at Heather's kitchen table and had a long overdue talk. Alice had no intention of moving into Aggie's house. She explained to Heather, "I've told your mother it would take me at least two months to get ready to move, but in the meantime I would take care of everything for her." She sipped her tea. "I know that old woman is up to something, and I have a feeling we'll soon find out what she's planning."

"I told your mother that by the end of two months," Alice continued, "we will have the orphan cats placed in good homes, and also find homes for George, Jasper, Peachy and Dilly, the four left behind."

Heather said, "She gets more unpredictable by the day. God knows what she's planning."

Alice refilled the teacups. "Heather, your mother was always unpredictable. Your father had his hands full keeping her on an even keel. Her odd ways just intensified after he died, that's all. Don't drive yourself crazy trying to figure her out. Besides, I think she thrives on being the town kook."

"She yelled at me the other day and said I was just like Arch. A control freak."

"You are like your father, who was a kind and responsible man. Most daughters would have bailed out by now. You just keep hanging in there. Now get a pad and pen so we can make up some smarmy ads to entice people to come and look at Aggie's orphans. Our first job is to get rid of those damn cats."

"You're right. Mom might feel differently if we find good homes for the cats."

Two days later, when Heather was doing her weekly grocery shopping, she decided to pick up a few treats for Aggie and Alice. She wanted an excuse to drop by to see how they were getting along unpacking and arranging Aggie's things in the new apartment. She had offered to help, but Aggie had said, "No thanks. We don't need you underfoot telling us what to do."

Alice met her at the door, a look of warning on her face. She whispered, "Do not get involved in this."

Heather found her mother curled up in bed, the patch work quilt wrapped tightly around her.

She glared up at Heather. "I hope you're satisfied now. Feather ran away. She hates it here, and so do I."

Before Heather could say a word, Alice passed her a cup of coffee. She said, "It's possible that when I went out to the balcony to shake out a couple of blankets, Feather dodged out there. We're on the first floor so she could have easily jumped through the wrought iron railing and scooted off."

Alice leaned down to put cream in Heather's cup and gave her a big wink, that said, "Go along with this."

Aggie sat up in bed. "I'm not blaming you, Alice. If my daughter and her no-good husband hadn't forced me to move here, this wouldn't have happened." She lay back and tightened the quilt around her neck. "And I'm not moving out of this bed until my Feather is found."

Heather wanted to say that Feather was likely making her way back to the house, but Alice was standing out of

Aggie's line of vision shaking her head. So Heather drank her cup of coffee and said her good-byes. At the door Alice whispered, "I'll call you tomorrow."

Heather didn't know what her mother was up to, but she knew it had to do with not wanting to sell the house.

The next evening Alice arrived just as Heather was about to go upstairs to bed. She pulled her inside. "Come out to the kitchen. Earl's gone to bed. I'll make us some herbal tea."

Alice said, "I haven't been in touch with you since yesterday morning because I wanted to sort out the Feather thing."

Heather put two mugs on the kitchen table. "Have you found Feather?"

"Feather didn't run off. She was carefully stashed in one of the other apartments. Seems like Aggie paid the tenant down the hall to take care of Feather for a few days."

"How in the world did you find that out? And why on earth would Mom do that?"

"Well, for starters, I was immediately suspicious when I arrived yesterday morning and your mother went into her mournful act. She said that the quilt was haunted, that she felt Feather's little feet walk over her through the night. I know her, and I know that if Feather really were lost, Aggie would be up and down every street in town looking for her."

Alice accepted the mug of steaming tea and continued. "It was sheer luck that I found out where Feather was stashed. I was walking down the hall to the garbage shute when I heard a cat meow. I knocked on the door, and a thin little white-haired woman answered, Feather in her arms."

"When I asked her about the cat, she told me she was

149

taking care of Feather for a few days for a new tenant- said Aggie offered her so much she couldn't refuse."

"What did Aggie have to say about all this?"

"I haven't told her I know where Feather is. I'm letting her act out her little drama. You're not going to believe the second act."

Alice drained her mug and held it out for a refill. "When I got to the apartment she was still wrapped up in that damn quilt, still in the jeans and shirt she was wearing yesterday. I told her I wasn't going to do a tap of work until she got up, showered and put on some clean clothes. She just went on and on about the patch work quilt being haunted."

Heather asked, "Oh, my God, Alice, do you think she's really flipped this time?"

"No, I don't think she's flipped. I think this stunt she's pulling is setting the stage for her to move back into the house and get us off her back about selling."

She held up a hand when Heather started to speak. "She's good. Her description of a cat walking up and down the quilt in the middle of the night gave me the creeps. She wants me to spend the night and sleep under the damn quilt. Aggie now claims that Feather is dead and her spirit has come back to haunt her."

"She must think we're a couple of dipsticks to believe that. Honest to God, Alice, I've had it with her."

Heather got to the apartment before Alice the next morning. She needed to be alone with her mother.

The first thing she said to Aggie was, "Did Feather's ghost come back again last night?"

Aggie pulled the quilt up under her chubby chin. "I just knew Alice would run and blab everything to you."

"Isn't that what you wanted her to do? Didn't you want me to know about Feather's ghost? Mom, I think living here is too upsetting for you, and that it would be better if you moved back to your house. I think that's what the haunting is all about. It's a warning for you to move back."

"You're one bitch of a daughter. Are you telling me you don't care if I leave here?"

"That's what I'm telling you, Mom. You can move to the damn moon, if that's what you want. Luckily you didn't take much furniture with you, so the move back won't take long."

Heather reached down and grabbed the quilt. She folded it carefully and put it on a chair. "Mission accomplished, Mom. Alice will be here any minute and there's something else I want to say before she gets here. 'I quit!'"

Aggie glared at her. "Quit what?"

"Everything. I quit trying to help you. Most of all I quit letting you suck me into all your craziness. I know you're old, and you're my mother, but I give up. From now on you're on your own. Do your own bloody errands, and do something about your own meals. I'm handing in my resignation."

"I always knew this would happen, that you'd never take care of me the way a decent daughter would. What would your father say about you now?" She pointed a plump finger at the door. "Take off! Who needs you anyway? Alice will take care of me!"

"There's a limit to what Alice will put up with. She's not your daughter."

Alice was standing in the doorway with Feather in her arms. "Heather's right, Aggie. There's a limit, and I've just about reached it."

Feather jumped out of Alice's arms and headed straight for the patchwork quilt. She jumped up on it and started to knead it.

"I want to go home," Aggie announced. "Today."

"Fine with us," Alice told her. She pushed Heather toward the door. "I'll call the movers and make all the arrangements. Go in peace. I'll talk to you later."

Heather whispered, "I'm going from here to Walker's Travel Agency. Earl wants to take off somewhere for a couple of weeks."

Pots and pans were being banged around in the kitchen. Aggie was grumbling to herself.

Alice gave Heather a good-bye hug. "Don't tell me where you and Earl are going. Please. Just relax and enjoy yourselves. Not having you at her beck and call will give your mother something else to growl about." Alice grinned. "To tell you the truth, Heather, I'm looking forward to her next kooky scheme." Then she turned and yelled at Aggie. "Easy on those pots, woman!"

MAKING DO

I t was that last moment before going to sleep, when she placed the bookmark in the book she was reading, placed the book on the night table, reached out to turn off the lamp, that Lois Scott felt lonely.

Her job at the town library was all-consuming. She loved everything about the job, the people sitting in the comfortable chairs reading, or working at one of the tables. She loved the organizing, the order, but most of all she loved the books.

Sometimes she thought her marriage to Des floundered because of books. At home, books spilled over every shelf and table. Early in the marriage, Des began making remarks about the stacks of books and the time she spent reading.

Whenever she suggested a book she thought would interest him, he would say, "You married a coal miner, my dear, not a reader."

She regretted his not being a reader of books. He was a great reader of newspapers, and he would discuss the news and editorials with a wonderful dry wit.

Her wish was that he would accept her spending so much time reading as part of who she was. She also wished that he believed her when she said she would be perfectly satisfied living in a miner's house, but it seemed to her senseless not to live in her family home.

Lois had met Des at a friend's wedding. She was aware of him watching her at the dance afterwards. Half way through the evening he asked her to dance. She liked him immediately. He was intelligent and warm, and best of all he was a wonderful dancer.

His way of asking her out was, "I suppose the town librarian doesn't date miners."

Her answer was, "My father was a miner and I certainly don't think I'm better than the woman he dated."

Now Des was out of her life and she was back to lonely evenings. Her best friend, who was also her closest neighbour, Glenna Richards, kept urging her to go out more, to learn to play bridge, to go to the church dances.

"And give everyone a whisper and a giggle over the sight of the thirty-five year old divorcee looking for another man?"

Glenna said, "I thought you don't care what people think of you."

It doesn't matter what people think of me. I've got a good life and I'm grateful for that."

"Jeez Lois, that's something I'd expect to come out of the wrinkled old mouth of my eighty-year-old Aunt Maude."

One Sunday afternoon in early March, Lois was tidying up the stacks of books in the living room. It was the kind of afternoon that demanded a fire in the fireplace. An icy wind had been pounding on the east side of the house all night and all day. She got a good blaze going before going to the kitchen to put the kettle on for tea.

Lois felt a pang of guilt about being so snug in her house, imagining her friend, Jean, getting into her clunker of a car to make the twenty-minute drive. Lois doubted that she would leave the comfort of her old house on such a day to have afternoon tea with a friend.

Lois was attached to her childhood home. She had actually been born in the big front bedroom. Her friend, Glenna, called the house "your safe hiding place." She and Glenna disagreed strongly about her using the house as a hideout from getting out there and finding herself another partner.

The friend who was coming for tea was a member of the study group Lois was running that winter. The topic was "The Lives of Women in Contemporary Fiction." The workshop proved to be one of the most successful ideas Lois had come up with to get more young women into the library. It also filled in one of her lonely evenings.

When Des had divorced her to marry a woman he had met on one of his fishing trips, Lois was more grateful than ever that her parents had willed her the family home. Des hadn't wanted to move into the house when they married.

He had accused her of being ashamed of living in a miner's house, of thinking herself better than the other miner's wives. That was far from the truth. Many of the women she had grown up with, and counted as friends, had married miners.

The house had been in the family a long time. Her father and mother had moved in with her grandparents during the depression, and the arrangement worked well. The old house on the edge of town was the only home Lois knew until she finished college and moved into an apartment of her own near the library.

Des never appreciated the house. He claimed the old place needed too much attention and that he thought their living there was the dumbest idea she ever had.

One of the things he had said to her when he left, was, "Now you can enjoy this damn old house in peace."

The separation was painful for her. Des had never made the earth move for her, but he had been comfortable to live with. He had a kind nature. She had liked being married and the hardest thing for her at first was that she had no one to cook for, to do things for.

She was grateful that she and Des hadn't had children, and that her job as town librarian kept her too busy to spend time feeling sorry for herself.

Lois was thinking about her friend Jean as she prepared the tea tray. She arranged slices of lemon loaf as she wondered if the things Jean was telling her about her marriage were true. Lois suspected that some of the stories were exaggerated.

One day Jean had said to her, "You're the kind of person I need as a friend. You're so easy to talk to, and I haven't had a soul to talk to about my rotten marriage.

Lois had looked at Jean's pale, unhappy face and asked

her bluntly, "Are you looking for a way out of your marriage?"

"There's no way out, Lois. Unless something should happen to Roger. God Forbid."

"Like what?"

"Oh, you know, a heart attack, or an accident."

"My God, is it that bad, that you're fantasizing about his death?"

Jean's voice was hardly above a whisper. "I think the only way out for me is if either of us were to die. Roger says he wants to be cremated when he dies, but I don't believe in cremation. I'd be afraid the soul might burn before it had a chance to leave the body."

"If Roger dies before me," she continued, " I'm going to bury him in the old graveyard down the road from where we live. His family has a plot there. I'd put his body in the ground, where it belongs, and put a headstone on his grave."

The look on Jean's face gave Lois the shivers. She couldn't get over the way Jean spoke so calmly of her plans for Roger's demise. She was arranging a linen cloth over the tea tray when Glenna tapped on the back door. Lois opened the door and pulled her in. "For God's sake, Glenna, get in out of that awful wind!"

She reached into a cupboard for a third cup and saucer. "Jean's coming over for tea. We're going to work on a workshop assignment. Alice Monroe's *Lives of Girls and Women.*"

Glenna rolled her eyes. "I'd rather have a root canal done than to sit here listening to you two moan about the lives of women." She took the cup and saucer out of Lois's hands and returned it to the cupboard.

157

"I'm making a butterscotch pie for supper and discovered I'm out of cornstarch."

Lois found the box of cornstarch. "Stay long enough for a quick cup of tea. Jean will be here any minute."

"Then I'm out of here. My God, Lois, I don't know how you can stand spending so much time with that one. She's so down all the time, she gives me the creeps. I wish you had never started that damn workshop."

"What a funny thing for you to say."

"Not so funny. You met Jean through that course. I think you're getting too involved with that woman's problems."

A few days later, Lois drove to Jean's house. It was Jean's fortieth birthday and Lois had baked her a cake. She also gift wrapped a blue scarf that she thought would go nicely with Jean's blue eyes.

Jean looked stricken when she opened the door and saw Lois standing there holding out the cake tin and gift bag. Lois stepped inside, put the cake and gift on the kitchen table and gave Jean a hug.

Roger, Jean's husband, appeared in the doorway between the kitchen and dining room. He took two long, slow strides toward Lois and held out a hand to her. "Nice to see you, Lois. Your brother Bob and I went to school together. You were a few grades ahead of us. Right?"

Lois was surprised at the warmth of the handshake and the friendly, pleasant voice. He was a tall, stocky man, and seemed very much at ease, hardly the man Jean had been describing the past several months.

But then no one would match Lois's description of her ex-husband with the Des that others knew.

"Bob and his friends trooped in and out so often in those

days," she said, "I could never keep track."

His voice changed when he spoke to Jean. "Aren't you going to offer Lois a cup of coffee?"

Jean moved to the counter where the coffee maker sat. She had yet to say a word.

Lois took the lid off the cake tin and held the chocolate cake out to her. "Happy Birthday, Jean!"

Roger grinned at her. "Now that's what I call a cake. I remember your mother's chocolate cake. Best darn cake in town. I bet this one's made from her recipe. Right?"

Later that evening, Lois tried to reconstruct the birthday visit for Glenna. "It was weird. Because Roger's trucking business is in Sydney, I haven't seen him around for a long time. When Jean had told me who she was married to I had a vague recollection of his being one of Bob's high school crowd."

Whenever Jean talked about Roger I pictured a rough, broody type," she continued. "Actually he was very friendly. Charming even."

"What were he and Jean like together?"

"They could have been strangers. We sat at the kitchen table, had our coffee and cake and chatted. I mean Roger and I chatted. Jean hardly said two words the whole time I was there."

When we finished eating, Roger stood up and said, "Nice of you to drop by Lois. Maybe I'll stop in the library for a visit one of these days."

"Wasn't that a strange thing for him to say?" Lois continued. "He just stood there, smiling at me, waiting for me to say my good-byes."

"Didn't Jean say anything, for God's sake?"

"She walked me to my car. Before I drove off she leaned into the car and whispered, "You shouldn't have come. I told you that Roger doesn't want my friends coming to the house.""

Glenna shook her head in disbelief. "If she's so unhappy, why the hell doesn't she just leave him and make a life for herself?"

Lois ticked the reasons off. "She married at seventeen. She has no education or job training. Roger refuses to allow her to work outside the house, and most significant of all, I'm sure she truly believes herself incapable of making a new life for herself."

"What about their daughter who lives in Halifax? Can't she help her?"

"Jean would love to move back to Halifax, She keeps talking about being a city person. But she said her daughter is married with problems of her own."

Glenna reached for the bottle of wine and refilled their glasses. "Tell me about their house. It's that old brick place half way into Sydney, off the airport road, isn't it?"

"That's the one. It's one of those old, two-story, Victorian houses. Much like this one. A beautiful property. Must be a whole acre of land. The place used to belong to Roger's family. The outside is well kept. The inside, the little I saw of it, looks as if nothing's been changed in fifty years. It's spotlessly clean, but the furniture is very old, and very worn."

"Well, all I can say is if Jean's as unhappy as she says she is, and if the marriage is as rotten as she claims it is, she's the only one who can do something about it."

Lois took a sip of wine. "Some time ago when I told

Jean about Des leaving me for another woman, she said, 'I should be so lucky. That would solve everything for me."

"Yeah. Well. I know you and Des didn't have a marriage made in heaven, kiddo, but I know his leaving still hurts."

"It's getting easier." Lois held up her glass. "Thanks to friends, and my job at the library."

That night when she was brushing her teeth and doing her nightly creaming, Lois thought about Des. She was remembering the night he had asked her out. She knew he was five years younger but it didn't seem to matter. She also knew, as did everyone else in their small town, that his wife had left him for another man. But at the time nothing mattered to Lois except how much she liked him. He made her laugh, And there was that dancing of his.

She was thirty years old when she met Des and hadn't had a man in her life for over five years. Lois had always liked men with a stocky build and a good sense of humour. Des had both.

Des leaving her had done something to her confidence. She didn't trust her judgement of men any more. She found herself shying away from any social gathering.

A few days after the birthday visit to Jean, Des was waiting for her as she closed the library. About once a month he would drop by and they would have a coffee together before they went home for supper. Until she and Des began to share the occasional coffee, Lois never believed that it was possible for divorced people to become friendly. She looked forward to their coffee visits and chats.

Des said he wanted to keep in touch, to see that she was O.K. Lois suspected that he was a bit lonely. His new wife had the reputation of never being home.

When they were settled in their booth at Tim Horton's, Lois said, "On your own again?"

Des stared into his cup. "Yeah. I'm getting a bit pissed off about Elaine being away somewhere at least two days of every week."

Lois smiled at him. "Don't be such a baby, Des. You're perfectly capable of looking after yourself."

"Good job I can look after myself. Elaine knows nothing about running a house. I didn't appreciate how you kept the household wheels greased with such little effort. I miss that."

"Is that why you married me? Because I was a good housekeeper?"

He started to laugh. "You were also soft and pretty and great company. That's when you didn't have your nose in a book.

But hey, here we are drinking coffee together and talking like a couple of old friends." He leaned over and gave her arm a little squeeze.

On the last night of the course, the library group decided they didn't want to lose touch and that they would continue to meet. They decided to meet once a month in each other's homes. Everyone was enthusiastic about the plan except Jean.

On their way home, Jean explained to Lois why she couldn't continue to be part of the group. "The only reason Roger allowed me to take this course was because it was being given at the library. I know he would never agree to my having the group at the house."

"For God's sake, Jean, you have to have friends. What's he going to do? Stand in the doorway and tell them they can't come in?"

"You don't think he'd do that? The only reason you got in the house on my birthday was that your arrival was a surprise."

"What are you talking about? Roger was very pleasant that day."

There was a sly look on Jean's face. She turned away. "He likes you a lot. When you left he said he should have married someone like you, not a city girl. He raved on and on about how I trapped him into marriage by getting pregnant, how I didn't fit into small-town life, how foolish he had been to marry me." She gave Lois a sidelong glance. "Did you find Roger attractive?"

Lois snapped, "No, Jean, I didn't find your husband attractive".

The minute the words were out of her mouth, she knew they weren't true. She had found Roger very attractive. She had even begun to fantasize about him. She liked the look of his stocky, solid body. She liked his thick, graying hair and she liked his deep, calm voice.

"Jean, you say that your only way out of the marriage is for Roger to meet someone else. That's magical thinking. For God's sake, just tell him you want out."

Jean stopped the car in Lois's driveway, and for the first time since the course began, Lois didn't invite her in for coffee.

Jean said, in a little girl voice, "You're cross with me, aren't you?"

The open car door flooded the inside of the car with light. Lois looked directly into Jean's eyes. "Jean, get some help."

Jean began to cry. "I've begged Roger to come to a marriage counsellor with me. He's like a wild man when I even mention it. I can't help it if I hate living in this town. I hate it. It's so damn boring. There's never anything to do."

"Get some professional help for yourself, Jean." Lois got out of the car and walked toward her house.

The next day Lois was taking her afternoon tea break when Roger arrived at the library.

"I was in the neighbourhood and just thought I would drop in and say hi. I enjoyed seeing you again." He acted as if they were old friends. She was in her small office and he made a move to sit on the chair beside her desk.

"Don't sit down Roger."

"Hey, Lois. Aren't you even going to check the teapot to see if there's enough left to offer me a cup?"

She stood up. "There isn't any tea for you, Roger." She walked him to the office door. She smiled and waited for him to leave, just the way he had smiled and waited the day of the birthday visit.

Lois didn't see Jean again for a few months. There were several phone calls. Lois was friendly, but had ready excuses why she couldn't go shopping or meet for coffee.

Another member of the workshop group told Lois about the birth of Jean and Roger's first grandchild, and about the baby clothes Jean had made, and how Roger had papered and painted a room in preparation for the baby's first visit.

The evening Lois and Glenna attended the town's Spring Fair was the first time Lois saw Jean since the last night of the workshop.

Roger was pushing the carriage. Jean had one hand on the carriage hood. Their daughter and son-in-law walked beside them.

Lois said to Glenna, "Let's turn and walk the other way. I don't want to talk to them."

Glenna took in the tableau before turning. "They look like a re-run of *"Father Know's Best"*, don't they?"

Lois nodded. "Maybe now Jean will get to visit Halifax more often."

"And maybe you and I will win this week's lottery and take a cruise to the Greek Islands. Come on, girl, I hear this year's fortune teller is a marvel. Let's go and find her tent."

Lois glanced over her shoulder for a last look at Roger pushing the carriage. She wondered what it would be like to be in Jean's shoes.

Aldershot Eng.

Oct 3-43

THE PAY-OFF

S ally and her best friend Jan, had brunch on Sundays with Sally's mother, Kate. The arrangement began years ago as a way for Kate and Sally to have a visit. Sally refused to see her father. She hadn't laid eyes on him since she was seventeen. Now, twenty-five, she intended never to see her father again.

Kate kept begging her to come home to visit Walter. "After all, Sally," she would say, "he's your father and he's not getting any younger."

Sally's heart had hardened against Walter when she was a small child. She had long ago accepted the fact that she hadn't fared well in the father department.

One day Jan said to Sally, "You turn sullen and sad

whenever the old bastard's name is mentioned. I wish to God you could put those years behind you."

Sally thought, *Not even Jan knows the darkest corner in my heart reserved for Walter. He beat the shit out of Ross and me countless times for some minor infraction of one of his friggin' rules.* Ignoring him was the only way she could get back at him. *She often wished she could get rid of her anger. She knew in her heart that her anger wasn't hurting Walter. It was hurting her.*

One morning in May, Sally decided they would have brunch at her apartment instead of going to a restaurant. They were eating pancakes and maple syrup as Kate began one of her round-and-round-the-mulberry bush conversations.

Kate asked Sally, "What if Walter had a terminal illness?"

There was a long pause. "I wouldn't go to see him if he were dying."

Kate began to cry. Sally rolled her eyes. "Ma, I think you must have a special tear button you push."

Looking younger than her fifty-five years, Kate had soft blonde hair, pale blue eyes, and a gentle face. The gentle face was the one she showed the world. Sally had seen her mother's face terrified beyond description the times she begged Walter to stop the beatings.

"Your father has a birthday two weeks from today. I'm not asking you to come home for a visit, Sally. I just want you to phone Walter and wish him a happy birthday."

Sally jumped up, ran to the apartment door and opened it. "Out Ma. You know what I told you. I won't have that man's name mentioned in my home."

Jan looked embarrassed as Kate continued to cry, dabbing at her eyes with an already wet tissue. "Dear, that's so heartless, not allowing me to mention your father."

Sally was weary of Kate's coaxing her to go home. She thought, *there she sits in her blue silk dress and double strand of pearls. She looks smart but pitiful, if you can look smart and pitiful at the same time. Why the hell didn't she make her escape when Ross and I left?*

With her wash-and-wear hair cut, her jeans and T-shirts, Sally's style was a strong contrast to Kate's. Yet, they looked like sisters. They had the same colouring and the same tall, thin frames.

Jan was looking uncomfortable, as she always looked when Sally was being rude to Kate.

Ignoring the open door, Kate rummaged in her bag for more tissues. "You refuse to see your father. Ross lives on the other side of the world. He never writes home." She blew her nose. "Although I know he writes to you because you read his letters to me."

"Make up your mind, Ma." Sally was still standing at the door. "Change the subject or leave."

"Please, Sally. Just phone and wish him happy birthday. That's all I'm asking. Please."

Sally put her hands over her ears. "I'm not listening, Ma."

Kate walked over to Sally. Their noses were almost touching as Kate enunciated each word carefully, "If you will call Walter and wish him a happy birthday, I will give you an all-expense paid trip to Scotland to visit Ross." Then she slipped past Sally, closing the door softly.

Jan was pouring more coffee when Sally rejoined her at

the table. "Can you believe that woman?" Sally yelled. When will she give up?"

"You're going to take that money, aren't you?" Jan asked. "I know how badly you want that trip."

Sally's twin brother was a potter in a Scottish Highland village. She hadn't seen him the past two years. "For sure I'm going to take the money. Knowing it's Walter's money that Ma has been squirreling away will make spending it all the more enjoyable."

Jan and Sally had been in and out of each other's homes since kindergarten. Jan's father was a wonderful man. One of the things Sally loved about Jan was that she was willing to share her dad with her and Ross. Even as small children, they were aware of the differences in their homes. Sally's home was all regimentation and tension, while Pam's family shuffled along at a loving pace.

Walter had been a drill sergeant in the Second World War, and he ran their home like a drill sergeant. Kate made excuses; his war injury, not being able to work in the mines again, having to live on a war pension. She made excuses, at the same time, she placated him. Anything to avoid his rages.

Sally believed that she and Ross could have put up with the regimentation. It was the name-calling and the beatings that filled her heart with darkness.

When they were children, Sally told Jan, "I pretended that my real life was at your house, that I only slept and ate my meals at Walter's house." Sally called her father Walter behind his back, called him nothing to his face.

Once, when they were in their teens, and Walter was being verbally nasty, Jan asked her, "How do you keep from talking back when he speaks to you like that?"

Sally answered, "Because he would hit me if I said a word. Anyway, Ross and I have only a couple of years left. Our escape is all planned. We're leaving when we graduate from high school."

That's exactly what they did. They had a rough time of it for a few years, living in a basement apartment, working weekends while they continued with their education. Jan's folks and an uncle helped.

Ross had managed two years at the Sydney College of Arts, and Sally and Jan attended a community college where they earned their early childhood diplomas.

Sally said to Jan, "Ma knows I can only afford a trip to Scotland every four or five years. She knows I would do anything for that plane ticket. She knows what buttons to push."

"Well?"

"Well what?"

"Are you going to go?"

"You bet your sweet ass I'm going." Sally jumped up, ran to Pam and hugged her. "Can you believe it? I'm going to see Ross! I'll go to the travel agency on my lunch hour tomorrow. I'll phone Ross and give him my flight number and time of arrival."

"Why not write him?"

"Because I'm going on the first available flight. Things are slow at the Day Care Centre. Besides I have loads of overtime saved."

That was the end of the conversation. Sally didn't want Jan to start in on her about how healing it would be if only she would get some help about her stuffed down anger.

Two Sundays later, Sally, Jan and Kate were at the Sydney Airport. Sally was holding out a hand to Kate. "The money, Ma. I put the ticket on my Visa, but I want the money you promised before I board that plane."

Kate passed her an envelope. "Walter's mad as a hornet because I left the house on his birthday. He said he wouldn't be there when I got back. Said he was going to go out and celebrate his birthday with someone else."

"That should be an interesting celebration, seeing he hasn't anyone in his life other than you." Sally signaled the waitress for more coffee.

Kate's cup rattled on its saucer. Her eyes darted around the restaurant. She pointed to the far wall. "There's a pay phone, Sally."

"When I've finished eating, Ma." Sally's mouth was full of toast.

Pam leaned over and whispered to Sally, "I hate that smug, secretive look on your face."

Kate was looking agitated and close to tears.

Sally was thinking, *She's my mother, and I love her, but I'm disappointed that she didn't have the guts to leave Walter. Sometimes I feel sorry for her. Other times she makes me crazy.*

"Your flight will be leaving soon, Sally," Jan said.

Kate reached across the table and touched Sally's face.

Sally gathered up her things and rushed out of the restaurant, Kate and Jan trailing behind her. She gave them each a peck on the cheek at the boarding entrance.

"There's a phone inside, Ma." Sally grabbed her mother and hugged her. "Ma, Ross and I thank you from the bottom of our hearts for this trip." She grinned at her best friend and was gone. She knew that Jan and her mother both knew that she had no intention of phoning Walter.

Kate fluttered her hands as she called after Sally, "If you call Walter, he'll never tell me." Then, her voice full of pleasure, she added, "Give Ross my love. I want you both to enjoy every minute of your visit."

The first thing Jan said to Sally when she met her at the airport on her return from Scotland was, "You won't believe what your mother said after you boarded that plane. Listen to this: "I can't wait to tell Walter that Sally is off to Scotland to visit Ross. He'll rant like a madman for days." Jan shook her head. "Sally, your mother looked downright delighted."

Sally smiled. "Ma has her own way of getting back at Walter."

On the drive home from the airport, Jan said "I can't wait to hear every detail of you're visit."

Sally said, "On the first hour of our visit, Ross said to me," "I know from your letters that your still hanging on to anger. So Walter was a rotten father. We had a good mother and good friends, and enough guts to get away from him."

Then he said, "Just imagine how pissed off he must be that we got ourselves an education, and we're doing well."

Sally put down her luggage and gave Jan a big hug. "It was like magic. Ross put everything in perspective for me. I know I'm finally ready to say good-bye to the beatings and name-calling. I'm wondering if Ma was hoping this would happen. I can't wait to tell her all the things Ross and I did on our visit, and I can't wait to give her the beautiful pottery Ross made for her." She hugged her friend again, "And wait until you see the gift he made for you."

REMEMBRANCE
OF LOVE

It was a warm spring day, a Tuesday, an ordinary day in Marie's life, her usual routine. Breakfast with her brother, a brisk walk to her school. It was the day that would change Marie's life forever.

Marie knew her life would never be the same. Until that day, in her thirty-five years on earth, she had not experienced evil. She believed it existed, but she herself had never come upon it. The person she loved most in the world brought the experience of evil to her.

If only she could erase that moment, the moment she pushed open her brother's study door, and saw him sitting in the corner leather chair, holding a young boy in his lap.

Her brother, her beloved brother, sitting there, fondling a young boy's genitals.

Shock silenced her. The boy's back was to her, and Thomas was leaning over, whispering something in the boy's ear. She backed away. The moment she took a step backwards, Thomas looked up and their eyes met.

She was still sobbing when he came to her room half an hour later. When he sat on the bed and reached out to touch her, she cringed. She sat up and moved away from him. "Don't. Don't touch me. Please don't touch me."

"Marie, we have to decide how to handle this." She was thinking, *Next to the day Gran died, this is the worst day of my life.* Her sense of loss was like the death of someone dear.

"What do you mean, handle this?" she yelled at him. She stood up and reached into her closet for a jacket. "I can't bear to be in the same room with you. I'm going out."

He followed her down the stairs. "Marie, what are you doing home in the middle of the afternoon?"

"I had one of my migraines. My principal covered for me so I could come home." She stopped and turned to face him. "Think of the irony, Thomas. I'm a teacher. I've had to deal with abused children." She felt sick with loathing. She couldn't bear to look at him. "I know more than I want to know about pedophiles. By the way, you're the first one I've met face to face."

He followed her out of the room and then collapsed on one of the stairs and put his head down on his arms. "You're going to report me, aren't you? Marie, I promise you it will never happen again. It wasn't meant to happen."

"I don't know what I'm going to do," she spat at him.

"Not long ago, one of my friends said she thought you were an arrogant bastard. I agreed with her that you could be arrogant at times, but never a bastard. God, I wish I were big and physically strong, I'd pound you senseless."

He sat there, his head on his arms, silent.

"Who was the little boy, Thomas?"

His words were muffled. "What does it matter?"

"What does it matter!" she screamed at him. "Jesus Christ Almighty!" She wished she had something heavy in her hands. She wanted desperately to smash him. "My God, Thomas, think of the damage. Think of his family. Tell me his name."

"Jamie Campbell. I wasn't hurting him. He was enjoying it."

Her mouth filled with bile. Jamie was an only child. His mother, Winifred Campbell, was a young widow, and an active member of St. Andrew's, taught a Sunday school class. Marie had worked on various church committees with Winifred and admired the way she was dealing with the loss of her husband. Marie told Winifred that one day, and she had replied, "I put on a good front, Marie, but to tell you the truth, if it weren't for having to keep up for Jamie's sake, I'd be a basket case. Having to take care of Jamie, and the support I get from our church, helps me to put one foot in front of the other and keep going. Your brother, Thomas has been so good to me. There isn't a week he doesn't stop by the house." Her face took on a kind of worshipping glow when she said Thomas's name, and Marie thought, *another woman in the congregation smitten with Thomas.*

Marie lurched out the door and headed in the direction of St. Andrew's. The church was situated on Ocean Drive, a quarter of a mile from the beach, and close to their old home. Some Sundays, if there was a high wind, the muted sound of the waves hitting the rocky shore could be heard over Thomas's sermon.

When Thomas became minister of St. Andrew's, Marie had been so proud. Sometimes, when she sat in church, listening to his wonderful sermons, she wondered what Gran would say if she were still alive. When they were young, she asked Gran why she was sometimes hard on Thomas, she answered, "Thomas acts too big for his britches. I take him down a peg or two to keep him grounded." Then she elaborated, "Your mother, may her soul rest in peace, doted on that boy to the point of obsession, especially after your father's death. I used to worry that your feelings were being hurt by all that attention going to Thomas, but you know, even at four and five, Thomas made a big fuss if you were left out. I can still hear him. Marie too!"

When she told Gran that she had no memory of her mother spoiling Thomas, Gran said, "You were only two when your dad died, and she was not herself ever after. She used to be so bonny when they were first married, then your father got the T. B., and the poor soul never had the inner strength to deal with the hardship of that. But she loved you. She loved you both. She just clung to Thomas to an unhealthy degree."

Gran's old house was close to the church, and when Marie reached it, she thought, If there is a way to live through this pain, this is the place I will find it. All of Marie's childhood memories were centered there. It had been Marie's house since Gran died ten years ago. She climbed the sagging front steps and sat on the wooden swing on the verandah.

Gran had left the old house to her, much to Thomas's chagrin. She rented it out a few times, but no tenant ever stayed more than a year. For a long time, Thomas nagged her to sell the place, but she refused. Marie had dreams of getting married and having a family of her own. She prayed for a strong, steady man who was handy with a saw and hammer, a man who would love her and help her fix up Gran's house. She had been twenty-five when her grandmother died, and now, at thirty-five there still wasn't anything she wanted more passionately than marriage and children.

She had come close to marriage once. She had been nineteen, back from her first year of college, happy to be home with Gran. Thomas had a summer job in Halifax that year, and while Marie missed him, she was glad he would be home only on weekends. She liked having Gran and the house to herself.

She found a part-time job at one of the local grocery stores as cashier, and was surprised to find, on her first day on the job, that her best friend, Kate, had a brother reporting for work also. Jim was seventeen and going into his final year of high school. He was planning to attend St. Francis the following year. According to Kate, Jim was the brains of the family and his parents expected him, as the oldest boy, to succeed at whatever profession he chose, and to set an example for the other five.

Marie liked all six of Kate's brothers, but Jim was her favourite. He was handsome, and funny, and popular. When Marie teased him about all the phone calls he got from girls, he teased her back. "How come I never get a phone call from you, Marie?" Then his voice became serious, "If I phoned you and asked you out, would you say yes?"

She was surprised at her reaction. "I'll take you up on that someday."

Kate said to her, "I think our Jimmy is sweet on you. Wouldn't it be something, Marie, if you became my sister-in-law? Then she laughed. "Naw, it could never happen. For one thing, Thomas would lock you up before seeing you married to a Catholic. You haven't got the makings of a Catholic anyway."

Marie asked her, "What do you mean?"

"You're determined to have a career. If you married a good Catholic boy, you'd be pregnant every other year. Somehow, I can't see you tied down with a bunch of kids."

No one was more surprised than Marie herself when she and Jim began dating. Marie had a reputation for being shy where men were concerned, but with Jim, the shyness disappeared. When she was with him, she felt her real self, or as Gran would put it, *No need to act the part.* Jim made her feel special, and she was grateful that she was having her first serious romance with such a kind, thoughtful person.

They shared a magical summer, full of trips to Mira for evening picnics, often dancing on the beach to music from a battery operated radio.

She and Jim began dating after attending a dance at the Mira Yacht club early June. They had often danced together before that night, and danced well together. That night was different. They danced every single dance, as if there weren't another soul on the dance floor.

Later, Marie tried to figure out what was so different between them on that first Mira dance of the summer. She thought, *maybe it was the full moon. Maybe it was the soft summer breeze. Maybe I was just ready.* At the end of a slow waltz, when Jim leaned down to kiss her, she closed her eyes and gave in to his closeness and the pressure of his mouth on hers.

When the kiss ended, Marie stood back and laughed. "Wow, you! Where did you learn to kiss like that?"

He grinned at her. "I've been practicing, and I've been looking forward to that kiss for a long time."

Kate and her partner danced by, and Kate called out. "Watch that guy, Marie. I wouldn't trust him as far as I could throw him."

Jim pulled her close. "I know you and Kate are best friends, Marie, and I know from your hanging out at our place so much, and our being around each other since we were little kids, you're not likely to take me seriously." He leaned down and kissed her again. "But I am serious. I want you to be my girl."

She said, "Jim, that's the most wonderful compliment I've ever had."

He held her tightly. "Year after next, I'll be in college. We can see each other every day. I can't wait to get away from the prying eyes of our families."

The rest of that evening they talked about places they would go and things they would do that summer. The next morning at work, Jim slipped her a note and whispered, "Read it on your break." It was the first of many love notes.

Marie expected resistance from Thomas, and she got it. The first weekend he was home, and found out she was dating Jim, he raved on as if she had taken up with a criminal. After that, he invited a friend home every weekend, someone he thought a more suitable boyfriend for his sister. Marie felt sorry for Thomas's friends, and tried to include them in the weekend parties and dances. She didn't want their visits to be a total loss.

Kate was a different matter. When Marie said to her, "I thought you would be pleased", Kate answered, "Well, I'm not, and I'll tell you why. Kid, you might be two years older than our Jimmy, but he's miles and miles ahead of you in experience. He's been chasing skirts since he was fifteen, and I happen to know that he's already experienced sex."

"Kate, don't you think I have enough sense to take care of myself?"

"I see the way you two are together, and it's worrying me. It's obvious that you're crazy about each other. I'm glad Jim has another year of school before he's off to college."

Marie looked back on those summer weekends as the happiest time of her life. Even Thomas's behaviour didn't spoil the fun for her. At the first of the summer, Thomas had insisted that she go to the weekend dances with him. Jim would have none of that. Every Saturday evening he would arrive at least an hour early to pick her up with some concocted story about something that he and Marie had to attend to before the dance.

When Thomas tried to keep Marie busy dancing with his friend and himself, Jim stood up to him. "Thomas, you're the best dancer in the hall," he said quietly, "so spread it around. There are at least ten gals standing around just dying for a dance with you. Marie happens to be my girl, and we're going to spend every possible minute together this evening."

When Jim led her out on the dance floor, he bent down

and whispered, "That brother of yours is a royal pain in the arse. Did you know that?"

Marie didn't disagree. "He's a bit overprotective at times. Give him time to get used to us as a couple."

Jim snorted. "Like he's going to give me a chance! I'm Catholic, and I'm in love with his sister. That's too much for him to swallow."

"Never mind, Jim. He's in Halifax all week."

Thomas never let up ranting about how much he disliked Jim. After one of his tirades, Gran remarked, "Is there a boy in this town you would consider a suitable beau for Marie?"

"Don't talk nonsense, Gran," was Thomas's answer.

When the end of her romance with Jim came, Marie was surprised when Thomas didn't gloat. Not one *I-told-you-so*.

Jim drove to Antigonish on a Sunday afternoon in late September to see her. He phoned ahead and asked Marie and Kate to meet him. Marie knew the minute she saw him that something was terribly wrong. They were sitting in the student centre, and when the waitress had served them coffee, Kate said, "What is it, Jim? God, but you look like you've lost your best friend."

He stared down at the coffee. "I've lost the best thing that ever happened to me. I've lost Marie." He looked at Marie, and tears ran down the sides of his nose. I've lost you, Marie." Then he turned to Kate. "You know I was going out with Dot Gillis before Marie and I began dating. Dot's pregnant. She just told me four days ago."

Kate stood up. "You two need to be alone."

"Please stay, Kate." Marie pulled her close. "Please stay."

One minute Kate would say something scathing and hurtful to her brother. "I thought you would have had enough sense to take precautions, you brainless twit!" Then she would lean across the table, touch him, and say something sympathetic. "I'm so sorry this happened, Jimmy."

Marie was the one to end the visit by telling Jim she wanted to drive back to Cape Breton with him. She wanted to skip classes for a few days. She knew what she really wanted was to be alone with Jim for a few hours, and then spend some time with Gran.

On the drive back Jim told her how both sets of parents and the parish priest ganged up on him. Marie thought about how Dot must feel. Dot was one of their crowd and Marie had always liked her. Jim cried again, but Marie was beyond tears.

When Jim talked about finding some way out of the mess, Marie told him, "I don't see a way out, Jim. I can't help thinking how Dot will have to give up her plans to take up nursing this fall. She must be devastated."

"She is. My parents and Dot's parents want me to continue my education. They want me to go to Nova Scotia Tech and get a degree in engineering. There are student quarters on campus there, plus Dot has an aunt in Halifax who has offered to help us." The last thing he said to her before dropping her off at Gran's was, "I did take precautions, Marie. I don't know how it happened."

The war had ended earlier that year. For Marie, losing Jim was another kind of ending for her.

Gran didn't act a bit surprised when Marie told her the news. "I know all about it Darlin," she said, "It would be no comfort to you right now if I told you it's likely all for the best." When she put her arms around Marie and crooned, "You're a bonnie lass, there'll be other boyfriends." Marie finally gave into tears. She cried for ten solid minutes, and Gran just held her, rubbing her back. *Oh, Gran, I wish I could tell you everything, what a wonderful person Jim is, how much I love him, and now he's going to belong to someone else. I can't tell you that we made love, because I know that would make you feel disappointed in me. But I'm not sorry, Gran. I can't confide in Kate either. It wouldn't be fair to Jim, and besides, she's upset enough as it is.*

She was thinking how fortunate it was that she hadn't become pregnant. They had taken precautions, but obviously that didn't always work.

"I'm going to make us a pot of good hot tea, my girl, and then it's off to bed with you."

"Oh, Gran, you think there's healing in your old tea."

"Yes, I do, hot tea, and turning your troubles over to God."

Marie did have other boyfriends after she lost Jim, but never one who made her feel that she was the only one for him, and that he was the only one for her.

Marie had wispy memories of her parents. Her father had died with T.B. when she was two and Thomas was seven. Her mother died a year later. Gran used to say she died of a broken heart.

The memories of her beloved Gran, even of the time her parents were alive, were stronger than her memories of her parents. That was likely because Gran had taken care of her almost from the time she was born. Every day, after her father's death, Gran would come first thing in the morning, get Thomas off to school, do the cleaning and laundry that had to be done, and prepare something for supper. It seemed to Marie that there was always a wonderful smell of home-made soup, bread or biscuits in that little kitchen. She remembered how Gran would coax her mother to eat.

If Gran had to go out on errands, she bundled Marie up and took her along. She told her years later, that her mother's emotional state was so precarious, that she was afraid to leave Marie alone with her.

Their grandmother was in her fifties and widowed when they moved in with her. She supplemented the meagre coal company pension she received by sewing and baking for others. There was good food and a comfortable home plus chores and lectures about duty and truth. Most of all there was love.

Gran didn't complain about her lot in life. She had several women friends who had also lost their men in the mines, and others whose husbands and sons were killed in the war. She referred to them as her *making-the-best of it* crowd. They kept boarders, did sewing and baking as Gran did, baby-sat grandchildren, and got together Saturday nights for a game of cards and some fancy sandwiches and cakes. They were the same women who kept the church clean and cooked the fund-raising suppers, and along with the other women in town, did Red Cross work, and knitting, and letter-writing to the men overseas during the war years.

Marie was careful to obey her grandmother's strict rules, but Thomas didn't. He stood up to her if he thought she was expecting too much of them. He was very protective of Marie and watched over her like an old hen.

It wasn't until Marie was in high school that she began to truly appreciate her grandmother. Part of it was Thomas's going off to Halifax to university, leaving Marie and her grandmother on their own. Every Sunday afternoon they would brew a pot of tea, and Gran would say, "Time for tea and gingersnaps, Marie. I want to hear all about your week. Don't leave anything out, now." Marie always got a smile out of her by replying, "I"ll tell you all about my week if you tell me all about your week."

Gran's gingersnaps. Of all the things Gran taught her to bake, the gingersnaps remained Marie's favourite because of those Sunday afternoon teas.

Marie was an excellent cook and homemaker by the time she was fourteen. Gran believed that cooking and keeping house were life skills that everyone should acquire. Thomas disagreed, resisting the efforts Gran made to teach him the rudiments. Thomas seemed to enjoy the clash of wills. He argued with Gran every chance he got. When he pointed out that she expected him to do all the outside chores, plus learn some housekeeping, she said, "Fair's fair. From now on Marie will help you bring the wood and coal in, and keep the yard tidy. She might have to do those things someday."

Gran finally gave up on the cooking, telling Thomas that with his looks and line of blarney, some silly woman would be there to wait on him. Marie thought, *Gran, you didn't know when you said that, that I would end up cooking Thomas's meals.*

Gran had refused to clean Thomas's room. Fortunately, he was fastidious about his clothes and surroundings, and kept his room clean. After Gran's death, he expected Marie to clean his room, but she refused. They quarreled about it. Marie's last words were on the topic were, "Thomas, I'm

187

not doing it."

He had laughed and said, "You sounded like Gran when you said that. Oh, well, you can't blame a guy for trying." Then he gave her a hug. "You know, Sis, I'm glad to see you acting assertive. I worry about you letting people take advantage of you."

Marie was thinking about those Sunday afternoons with Gran as she got up from the old wooden swing and walked over to the window of the front room of Gran's house. She rubbed one of the sleeves of her jacket across the dirty pane and peered in. Just looking in she was filled with memories of the happy times she had there.

She wondered what her grandmother would have said about Thomas's betrayal of the trust of that little boy and his mother. She was glad Gran wasn't alive to know about it.

When Marie was sixteen and Thomas twenty, Gran told them their mother had died of an overdose of sleeping pills. Thomas was in his second year of university by then, and had made his decision to go into the ministry. Gran felt they were old enough to know the truth, and that it was her duty to tell them the truth about the suicide. Gran lived her life by duty and truth.

On Thomas's eighteenth birthday Gran told them about the educational policy left by their father. The amount was to be divided between Thomas and Marie, and used toward their education. Thomas insisted that he should have the full amount. His reasoning was that Marie wouldn't be going to university. He said, "Better that she take a business course. She'll only end up getting married, anyway. Besides, university would be too difficult for her."

Gran, you knew without my telling you that I wanted to

go to university, too, didn't you? Thank you for not letting Thomas have my share of the money.

It had hurt Marie that Thomas wanted her share. She was a plodder and had to work twice as hard as Thomas for her good marks, but that didn't mean she wasn't a capable student.

Gran told Thomas, "You already have that scholarship. Your share of the policy will supplement that."

Thomas replied, "I could live more comfortably in Halifax if I had the full amount."

"Thomas, you're far too fond of the comforts of life for your own good," Gran warned.

With that, Thomas had slammed out of the house. Gran had been peeling apples for a pie. She put the paring knife down and turned to Marie. "My girl, you are not to live in Thomas's shadow."

Marie picked up an apple and began to peel it. "Oh, Gran, you know Thomas wouldn't want me to live in his shadow. You know how he includes me in everything, encourages me to be the best I can be. My girlfriends all envy me, having a brother like Thomas."

Gran gave a loud snort. "I've noticed how wonderful the girls think Thomas is. You've already forgiven him for saying university would be too difficult for you, haven't you?"

"He's my brother, Gran. He's good to me and I love him." She passed her grandmother the peeled apple. "But that doesn't mean he gets my share of the policy. I fully intend to go to university when I finish high school."

Two years later, when Thomas announced he was going to become a minister, Marie said, knowing how deeply religious her grandmother was, "Gran, you must be happy about Thomas's decision."

Her grandmother had frowned, then sighed, "I have some reservations about that, my girl. I have some reservations."

Marie wished now she had asked her grandmother to explain those doubts, as she walked around the back of the house to get the key she kept under the dilapidated flower box on the kitchen window sill. She opened the door, went in and sat at the kitchen table, the same kitchen table where she and Gran used to have their Sunday afternoon teas.

When Marie had moved into the manse with Thomas, she had taken with her the maple bedroom furniture, the oak dining room table and chairs, the lamps, and Gran's good china. Thomas had been annoyed. He wanted her to sell those things and use the money to buy new furniture for the manse. She didn't bother explaining to him that she thought of Gran's furniture as part of her dowry, if and when she married.

She drew circles in the dust on top of the old pine table in an effort to still her trembling. She felt broken inside, the way she had felt the day she heard about how her mother had died. She was glad Gran wasn't alive to know about Thomas, but at the same time she longed to have Gran beside her to comfort her, to advise her what to do.

There was no doubt in Marie's mind what advice her grandmother would give if she were alive.

No question about what has to be done, my girl. Do your duty to your church, to the community. Thomas must be made to leave the Church. Tell the truth, my girl. Tell the truth. Marie imagined with horror the effect of disclosure on Jamie's mother, St. Pauls, the town. The scandal would be immediate and disastrous.

She knew the research on pedophilia. It was likely Jamie wasn't Thomas's first victim, and wouldn't be his last. The chances of rehabilitation were not good. She couldn't let her mind deal with all that at that moment. Yet, thinking about anything else was next to impossible.

Thomas pushed open the back door, holding a large thermos out to her. "I knew you'd be here. I made us some tea." He reached into the pockets of his windbreaker for two mugs.

"You forgot the gingersnaps," she said.

When he looked blank, she realized he had likely forgotten about her Sunday tea and gingersnaps with Gran.

"I've been sitting here, communing with Gran, asking her if she thought it was my duty to tell the truth."

He poured steaming tea into the mugs. "Marie, don't go on about Gran and duty. You have to think about what will happen to me if you tell. I would be ruined. Finished. You can't do that to me. I'm your brother. I've been a good brother to you. I have always taken care of you, haven't I?"

She stared at his dark, handsome face. There were times when she had made excuses for Thomas. This time she knew she wouldn't do that.

Thomas began to drone on about where she should place her loyalties. Finally, she put her hands to her ears and started to yell at him. "Stop! Just shut up and get out of my house."

She had lots of practice in avoiding his angry moods, but for the first time she was unafraid when his face turned blotchy red.

He stood up, towering over her. "How dare you order

me out of this house! This place is as much mine as it is yours."

"If you won't leave, I will." She pushed back the chair and stood up to face him. Then she told him, "No, I'm not the one who is going to leave. Gran left this house to me. Thomas, what you've done is despicable. Before you leave my house, tell me one thing, when you say your prayers at night, do you discuss your sick behaviour with God?"

The next morning, when she awoke, the sun was shining through the half-opened venetian blinds, another sunny spring day. She buried her head in the pillow and sobbed.

She chanted to herself the morning litany her grandmother had taught her, *Every day is a new beginning, every day is the world made new.*

She remembered the moment she opened the door of Thomas's study yesterday. *Oh, Gran, you told me so many times that everything that happened to us in life, even the bad things, happened to teach us. What lesson am I to learn from this horror?* She buried her head under the quilt. More tears. She thought she had shed them all. She thought, *Every day is the world made more wicked.*

Then she heard her grandmother's voice in her head. *One rotten apple doesn't spoil the barrel. Get up and face the day. Do what has to be done.*

Her breakfast toast and cereal tasted like cardboard. She was rinsing out her coffee mug when Thomas appeared.

He stared at the empty coffee maker.

"I made myself an instant."

He scowled, his face flushing dark red. "Marie, you always make my breakfast."

"Well, I'm not going to make your breakfast ever again,

Thomas. Nor your lunch, nor your dinner."

"Marie, I have a board meeting in half an hour."

"Lots of time for you to make your own breakfast."

She didn't respond to his, "You know I can't cook."

Marie loved teaching. It didn't matter if it was standing in front of the children teaching a lesson, gathering her grade two class around for story telling time, answering their endless questions, playing games with them when she was on yard duty, listening to their problems, she loved every minute she spent with the children.

The next day was Saturday and Marie wanted desperately to see Kate, but decided she was too fragile to do that yet. To avoid Thomas's presence, she got up early, filled the trunk of her car with cleaning supplies, a bucket and cleaning rags, and drove to Gran's house.

It was going to be hard to tell Kate about what happened, to put words to the turmoil and sadness in her heart, but she knew Kate was the one person in the world she could turn to.

By one o'clock she was exhausted. She spent the whole morning scouring the kitchen. Every shelf, every drawer, the old stove and fridge, and the tiled floor was spotless. She planned to stock some groceries and prepare her suppers there. Breakfast could be managed before Thomas was up. She ate lunch at her desk or at the coffee shop in town. Supper was the one meal that needed planning.

She looked down the road to see if Thomas's car was parked in its usual place at the side of the church. He spent Saturday afternoons in the church study, preparing for Sunday.

She told Kate over the phone that she couldn't meet her

at Wong's for their usual Saturday night treat of Chinese food. She gave her friend a true excuse. "I'd be rotten company, Kate."

"Sure something better hasn't come up?" Kate asked. "Like an honest-to-God-man?" They had a running joke that their Saturday date would, of course, be cancelled if an honest-to-God-man turned up for either of them.

Kate had an apartment of her own near the Catholic high school where she taught history. Kate's family home was next door to Gran's old house, so the friendship had been solidly cemented before they even began school. Marie had spent part of every day of her childhood at Kate's place. She loved the happy noise of the place, caused mostly by Kate's six younger brothers.

The Protestant school and the Catholic school were a ten-minute walk, in different directions, from Ocean Drive. Each school day Marie and Kate met and walked home together. There was never enough time to say all they had to say to each other. Working out a scheme so they could be together while doing their chores, they convinced Marie's grandmother and Kate's mother that if they worked on the chores in each house as a team, the work would be done quicker and more efficiently.

Gran thought it was a great idea. She laughed at their request and said, "I'll have two for the price of one." Kate's mother didn't care one way or the other. Any help with running a house with seven kids in it was welcome.

Thomas never liked Kate, and Kate never hid her dislike for Thomas. One day Grandmother overheard Thomas say to Marie, "I thought you'd stop playing with that little Mick next door once you started school. Here you are in grade five and you still haven't made any Protestant friends."

Gran had been angry with him. "You think you can boss Marie about every little thing, Thomas. Well, I'm here to tell you to keep your nose out of Marie's choice of friends. Just because you're in high school now, don't think that makes you an authority on everything." Then she turned to Marie, "The friendship you and Kate have is special. It's going to be a life-long friendship. Remember that."

Marie never felt intimidated by her stern-faced grandmother. She was grateful for Gran's taking a stand whenever Thomas made some disparaging remark about Kate and her family. Gran was right about how important the friendship was to Marie. Kate was everything she wasn't, outgoing, full of confidence, brave about taking chances. When Marie said to Kate one time, "If I hang around with you long enough, maybe some of your easy ways will rub off on me," Kate had replied, "Be yourself, kid. You're fine, just the way you are."

When Kate decided to attend St. Francis Xavier College on the mainland, Marie had asked timidly, "Do they take Protestant students?"

Kate had roared with laughter. "If you got the money, honey." Then she became serious. "Talk to your grandmother, Marie. Wouldn't it just be the absolute end if we could go to the same university? Even if your Gran agrees, you know Thomas will do everything he can to prevent it."

Gran thought their going to the same university was a great idea. It wasn't that far from home, Marie and Kate would be together, and it was less expensive than Dalhousie.

Thomas flew into a rage when Marie told him her plans.

Gran said to him, "Thomas, you had the freedom to choose, why can't Marie have that also?"

Thomas blamed Kate's influence, and warned Marie that no good would come of her going to a Catholic university. He didn't speak to either of them for weeks, and for months afterwards, he would get up and leave the room when Kate appeared.

The Sunday morning after the quarrel with Thomas, Marie slipped out of the house before he was awake, and headed for her house. She planned to clean the bedroom she was going to sleep in.

Three hours later, satisfied with the scrubbing and waxing she had done, she put away the cleaning things and hurried to her car. She planned to change her clothes and head for Kate's before Thomas returned home from church, but she didn't quite make it. He was striding up the front steps just as she was about to leave. She knew by the colour of his complexion that he was in one of his rages. He pushed her back into the house.

She looked him at him with fresh disgust. "I told you never to touch me again."

He glared at her. "If you hadn't planned on attending church this morning, you could have at least had the decency to let me know so I could have answered people's questions after church. Everyone wanted to know where you were!"

When she tried to get past him, he grabbed her and pushed her into the living room.

She was astonished at her own anger. "I'm warning you, Thomas. Keep your rotten hands off me. If you pull or shove me once more, I'm going to pick up the first heavy thing I can find and smash you across the face. And you can get used to my not showing up in church as I don't plan on attending St. Andrew's again as long as you're in the pulpit. For one thing, I couldn't bear looking at the faces of the young boys in the choir."

She adjusted the straps of her shoulder bag and started out the door. He grabbed her roughly and pulled her back. "I won't have this, Marie. I won't have the congregation gossiping about your not being in church. What are people going to think?"

She stumbled down the front steps and into her car. "It's kind of late for you to be concerned about what people are going to think, Thomas!" she yelled at him before slamming her car door. She had to talk to Kate. She was going to come unglued if she didn't talk to Kate.

When she saw Thomas running down the driveway after her, she quickly pressed the lock button. When he motioned for her to wind down her window, she shook her head. He pressed his face close to the driver's window and mouthed the words, "If you tell Kate, I'll never forgive you. Never."

She turned the ignition key. As she pulled away, she rolled down the window and called back to him. "Strange how often the word forgive turns up in your sermons."

It was a warm morning. Several neighbours were sitting out on their front steps. Marie drove by, giving them a wave. She glanced in the rearview mirror to see Thomas standing in the driveway waving also.

Kate had been expecting her. She was making a salad for their lunch when Marie arrived. "My God, you look terrible. Did someone die?"

Marie slumped down on one of the kitchen chairs. "I

wish it were as simple as someone dying." When she blurted out what had happened, Kate just stood there staring at her, the sharp vegetable knife in her hand.

Marie was staring at the knife. "If that little boy were mine, I'd want to ram that knife into Thomas's guts."

Kate dropped the knife and rushed to her. She put her arms around her and rocked her back and forth. Then she pulled Marie to her feet and led her into the living room. "I've got the coffee made. We're going to have a cup laced with some good Irish Cream."

A few minutes later, when Kate returned with the coffee, Marie said to her, "You don't seem shocked, Kate."

"Of course, I'm shocked. Who wouldn't be? But my main feeling is grief for you. What in the hell are you going to do?"

"My first thought was to move away. Maybe Halifax. But that wouldn't solve anything."

"You're damn right it wouldn't."

"But I need to talk to someone at the church head office. There must be some kind of procedure they follow in these circumstances. Could you come with me?"

"You know I will."

"I want to move out of the manse as soon as I can manage it. I've already scoured the kitchen and one of the bedrooms in Gran's house. Are you game to help me paper the front room and the bedrooms?"

Marie covered her face with her hands and started to cry. "I try not to think of that dear little boy, Kate. My God, do you think I should go to his mother? I'm so ashamed, Kate. I'm so ashamed. To think my brother, the brother I thought so wonderful, could do such a vile thing, that someone I loved so much could be so sick."

Kate held her and comforted her. "You'll do what has to be done, Marie. It's going to be difficult, but if you can save one boy from being molested, it will be worth it."

"Marie," she continued. "Did you tell Thomas you're moving out?"

"Not yet. That's going to set him off." She told Kate about not cooking his meals and not going to church. Kate pulled her up and led her to the kitchen. "You can talk while I set the table."

For three days Marie managed to avoid Thomas. She and Kate went directly from their jobs to Gran's house, getting it ready for paper and paint. Thomas was out attending evening meetings, so Marie was settled in bed before he got home.

On the fourth morning he was up, drinking coffee when she came into the kitchen. He nodded toward the coffee maker. "Help yourself."

"I don't have time this morning," she said quickly. "I'm just going to make a sandwich and leave. I'll have a coffee when I get to school."

"What's going on, Marie? Someone told me that you and Kate have been at the old place every evening this week. People are beginning to talk. You'll have me thinking there's something strange going on between you two."

"Like we're a couple of lesbians? I had begun to think that you were gay, and I imagine other people assume that too. A handsome guy like you with dozens of women panting after you, even a few of the married ones, and here you are living with your old maid sister."

She was amazed that he made no reply. She was even

more surprised at how easy it was for her to say what she wanted to say to him, after spending so may years sitting at his feet. Even when he was so rotten about her dating Jim, she still looked up to him as her older, protective brother.

When she finished her sandwich, she turned to him and said, "Here's further grist for the gossip mill. Kate and I are taking a holiday together over the spring break."

"But you and I always take a spring trip together."

"That's right. But that's no longer possible, is it?"

Also, Thomas, I'm moving out."

His voice was full of anguish. "What is it you want me to do, Marie? What do you want me to do?"

She spoke quietly. "I want you to leave the church. I want you to seek professional help. I want you to leave this town."

Her calmness surprised her. He got up, grabbed the jacket on the back of his chair and slammed out of the house.

The following day the letter arrived. Marie had never before opened a letter addressed to Thomas. She had come home from work early to pick up a few boxes she had packed the evening before, and she wanted to get away before Thomas returned from his Wednesday afternoon meeting.

When she sifted through the day's mail and saw the letter, she tucked it in her jacket pocket. There was no "Reverend" before Thomas's name. Marie recognized Winifred Campbell's handwriting.

Marie made herself a cup of tea, sat in her grandmother's old rocker, and opened the letter.

The letter had no salutation. It read, *"Last Monday*

Jamie told me what you have been doing to him. I felt more horrified than I felt the day my husband was killed in the car accident. Jamie had been having nightmares and an upset stomach for some time. Monday, I found out why. He was home from school, sick with a stomachache. I gave him a scrapbook to look at, the one I had made for him when he was a baby, thinking it would amuse him.

As he looked at the pictures, he began to cry. At first I thought it was the snapshot of his dad playing with him that upset him. Then he told me. He told me you have been sexually molesting him for three months.

I held my darling boy in my arms and we cried together. When he told me you said you wanted to take his father's place, that this was a secret thing that fathers and sons did, I wanted to kill you for seducing my son, my wonderful, ten-year-old son.

I have been going over and over in my mind how such a thing could have happened. You were in and out of our home, our safe and loving home. You were our long time trusted minister. How could I have known what you are? You have betrayed everything I believed in."

You were counselling me, supposedly helping me get over my husband's death. You picked a vulnerable place to practice your betrayal, didn't you?

My first instinct was to confront you. It's important that you know that I know. I planned the conversation in my head. I was going to tell you, "My son is hurting and we both have to go into therapy because of you. I hope your soul rots in hell for all eternity. I hope that for the years you have left on this earth, you never have one minute's peace of mind."

The confrontation didn't happen. My family doctor warned me that you would deny everything, that the fallout from such a confrontation would be too hard for me to handle. He arranged therapy for Jamie and me.

I need help in deciding how to tell other parents of young boys in our congregation about you. I can't talk to anyone yet, but I feel I have a responsibility to other parents.

I know that the sadness in my heart will be there forever, but I also know that I don't have to confront you to let you know that I know what you've done to my son. I believe your secret will be out. My doctor says the healing will come when the secret is out. To think you are walking the streets, respected, enjoying the perks of being a man of the cloth. I want that all to end for you.

Marie folded the letter and carefully put it back in its envelope. She wanted to hand the letter to Thomas, watch his face as he read it, but she wasn't going to do that. She would show the letter to his superiors.

In the meantime she would go to Winifred and tell her that she knew. She would tell Winifred her plans to let Thomas's superiors know. She would ask her permission to keep the letter from Thomas until she spoke with his superiors.

Draining her teacup, Marie thought there was no point in cooking supper. She wouldn't be able to eat it. That evening, when she was sure Jamie was in bed, she would visit Winifred.

She put the letter in her purse, and said a silent thank-you. It was the impetus she needed to help her do what had to be done.

Gran, stay beside me, please. I need your strength. I need your wisdom to help me to do what must be done, I need the memory of your love to get on with life without my brother.

The Thomas she used to know was as dead to her as if he had fallen off the edge of a cliff. She imagined his broken body on the rocky reef, the reef slimy with sea moss, the same rocky reef where they had hunted tiny snails when they were kids.

The next day was Saturday, and Marie planned to spend it shopping for things she needed for the house. Kate was buried in spring report cards, so she was on her own.

By three o'clock, exhausted, but satisfied with all she had accomplished, she decided to go to the manse and pick up the bedding she had packed. She planned to spend her first night away from the manse that very night. Thomas spent most Saturdays in the church study, so she was surprised to see his car in the manse driveway. There was a second car there. Marie recognized it as Ruth Martin's. Her first thought was the gossip that Kate had passed on during their phone visit that morning, "Heard that Thomas and Eleanor Martin are becoming an item. One of the teachers on my staff said they were seen together in a restaurant in Sydney. You don't think Thomas would pretend to be serious about someone, do you?"

Marie smiled into the phone, "If Thomas were going to do something like that, Eleanor Martin would be an unlikely prospect. He can't stand her mother. Ruth Martin has been a thorn in Thomas's side from day one. Add to that, Eleanor isn't the type of woman Thomas pays any attention to. She's beautiful but not very bright."

For a moment, Marie thought of driving on by. *What the heck, I'll say a polite hello, gather the things I need in my bedroom, and slip out the backdoor.*

Marie assumed that Ruth was there to bend Thomas's ear about one of her everlasting church projects, but when Marie stood in the livingroom doorway, she saw that Thomas and Ruth and Ruth's daughter, Eleanor, were having afternoon tea. The table was set with one of Gran's lace cloths, Gran's Royal Albert china, and a silver tray of chocolate cupcakes.

Eleanor reached for the teapot, "Come have tea with us, Marie. I'm just going to pour."

Thomas waved her in. "Come and join us. I was telling Eleanor the other day that you were moving into your own place and I was going to have to manage on my own. Wasn't it thoughtful of Eleanor and Ruth to drop by with my favourite cupcakes?"

Ruth Martin was Marie's least favourite person in the congregation. She fancied herself the town matriarch, and because she had both money and clout, many people accepted the role she had assigned herself. Marie often felt a twinge of pity for Eleanor, with her soft, gentle air. It was rather pathetic to see a woman of twenty-five seeming to exist to do her mother's bidding.

They were both tall, slim women, but there the resemblance ended. Ruth was groomed and coiffed and turned out like a Madam of the Board, where Eleanor always looked as if she were modeling for Seventeen Magazine.

Marie wanted to wrench Gran's gold leaf china teapot away from Eleanor and to tell her, *Run, girl, Don't let Thomas use you. Don't let that mother of yours let Thomas use you.*

The minute Thomas opened his mouth, there wasn't a doubt in Marie's mind what he was up to. Marie wondered how far he would go. She held out the cup of tea Eleanor offered. "That teapot was my Gran's favourite possession. Her mother brought it with her when she came to Canada as a bride." She couldn't bring herself to look at Thomas.

Ruth spoke, "I was just asking Thomas when you planned to move." The unspoken question in her eyes was, *and why?*"

"I'll be moving into Gran's house any day now. I thought if I weren't here, Thomas would do something about his single state. I have a sneaking suspicion that he has a girlfriend tucked away in Sydney. Isn't that right, Thomas?"

Ruth's face turned from sweet to sour in a second, and Thomas almost choked on his tea. "My sister has a wicked sense of humour, Ruth. She's teasing. She knows how much I think of Eleanor."

Marie put her teacup down and excused herself. She couldn't stay in the room another minute. The pleased look on Ruth's face, and the lovesick glow in Eleanor's eyes as she passed Thomas the cupcake tray, were too much.

The next morning, Marie phoned Kate and told her to put the report cards aside for a couple of hours and come over to share the first breakfast in Gran's home. "I'm serving waffles, sausages, and maple syrup," she said.

"I'm on my way," was Kate's reply.

Marie described the tea party to Kate. Kate, her mouth full of waffle, shook her head, then she started to laugh. "Sorry kid, I know this is serious, but I'm trying to imagine

Ruth Martin as Thomas's mother-in-law. What happens now?"

"I have to have it out with Thomas. He has to know that I intend to go to the Halifax Seminary. My God, Kate, I can't stand thinking about his dark side".

"Marie, I don't think Thomas is a villain in his own eyes. Right now he'd do anything to protect his public image. He's likely frantic that you are serious about disclosing his behaviour." Kate paused and held her coffee mug out for a refill. "There's something I want to ask you. You've never mentioned going to the police. Have you thought about it?"

"All the time." Marie moved her plate, put her head down in her arms, and started to cry. "And I live in fear that Winifred Campbell will go that route. The evening I visited her, she talked about reporting Thomas to the police, but she feels my horror about going public. Christ, Kate, do you see the irony here. Child abusers have their secrets protected by their victims and the victims' families because of the pain and embarrassment that public disclosure causes. Winifred talked about that, but I had the feeling that if she had the inner strength to do so, if she weren't so worried about the effect of public disclosure on Jamie, she would have gone to the police."

"Marie, there's another thing I want to ask you. Do you somehow feel connected to Thomas's behaviour? Do you feel any responsibility?"

"I feel shame, Kate. Shame is what I'm feeling. I feel such overwhelming shame. And I feel disgust and disappointment. You know how people say, "I'm glad so and so isn't alive to know this?" Well, I'm glad Gran isn't alive to know what's happened." She straightened up and wiped her face with her napkin. "At least I can be grateful for that."

"There's something else you can be grateful for, my friend."

"What's that?"

"When this is all over, when time and prayers have helped you heal, you'll be your separate self."

"What do you mean, my separate self?"

"Thomas has always had power over you. When you were younger, I used to watch helplessly as you did everything to please, to placate, be what Thomas wanted you to be. You used to worry about the tension between your Gran and Thomas. Well, I think that was all about your grandmother trying to pry you free of Thomas's influence. Do you remember her telling you once that the best thing that ever happened to you was going to Antigonish, that those four years were breakaway years for you?"

"I remember." Marie started to clear the table. "And I remember what she said when I was trying to make up my mind about something. "If the decision comes from your heart, you'll know it's the right decision."

"When are you going to talk to Thomas?"

"I phoned and asked him to come over today. He was sarcastic, pointing out that for most people, Sunday was a church day. He hates my not attending church, and Kate, I really miss church, but there is no way I could sit there listening to him preach."

"I had better get back to my pile of report cards. I don't want to be here when he arrives. I've only seen Thomas once since you told me. We were both walking down Main Street, and when he saw me he crossed over to the other side. He wouldn't be thrilled to find me here."

When Kate left, Marie curled up with the mystery paperback she was reading and waited for Thomas. At two she made a pot of tea. At three she decided to phone the manse. Getting no answer, she gave up waiting. She knew he wasn't coming, and that he wasn't going to phone to tell her he wasn't coming.

Marie awoke the next morning to the sound of howling wind. Rain was coming down hard on the tin roof of the old house. She pulled a heavy sweater over her pajamas and went downstairs. The wind was blowing so hard, she didn't hear the kettle come to a boil on the kitchen stove.

She was still in her pajamas, eating breakfast when Thomas called. He wanted to come over and talk to her before she left for work. "I'm not going to school today. I have a bad cold," she told him. "I'm working on reports here at home, so come over anytime that's convenient for you."

He arrived an hour later. When she heard him shaking out his raincoat in the back porch, she pushed the stack of file folders aside, so they could sit at the kitchen table. When she offered him coffee, he nodded and sat down heavily.

Marie had never before seen her brother look unkempt. He hadn't shaved. She had never seen him in wrinkled clothes, clothes mismatched and looking as if they didn't even belong to him. He sat there, not speaking, drinking the hot coffee in gulps.

When he finally spoke, his dark eyes were piercing. "You meant it when you said you weren't coming back to St. Andrew's, didn't you?"

She nodded.

"And you must know the church gossips are having a hay day."

"Gossip is the least of my concerns, Thomas."

He slammed his empty mug on the table. "Do you think I'm the only flawed soul in this town? I could tell you the names of people in this town harbouring unspeakable secrets. I would have to sit at this table all day to list them. Would you like the names of those in my parish who are in the midst of adulterous affairs? Would you like to know about one of our elders who is inches away from being charged with extortion? Closer to home, how about your friend Kate's brother, Jim? He's an old boyfriend of yours, isn't he? Do you know he's become a lush? Two of my flock have had affairs with him."

She put her hands over her ears. Her voice was a whisper when she spoke. "Not one of those people is my brother, Thomas."

"If I weren't your brother, would you hate me less?"

"Thomas, I don't hate you."

"Then why are you acting so hateful toward me?"

"Thomas, this isn't about how I'm acting. We have to talk about what I have to do."

"You've quit coming to church, you've moved away from me. What's next?"

When she began telling him about Winifred's letter, her visit with Winifred, and her plans to go to his superiors in Halifax, his eyes were closed, his face white.

"I know you've told Kate. I know that from the way she looked at me when I saw her on the street the other day. And now I know you've talked to Winifred. That's why she slammed the receiver in my ear when I called to see why she hadn't been coming out to church. Who else have you talked to?"

"I've been talking a lot to Gran's spirit."

His face contorted with anger. "Gran monitored my every breath and act when she was alive, and now she's haunting me from the grave."

"Thomas! How can you think of her in that way? What would our lives have been like if we hadn't had Gran?"

"You've really bought into the family mythology, haven't you, Marie? Gran, the rescuer, hovering over us ceaselessly. If she hadn't hovered over our mother so anxiously, practically spoon-feeding her after Dad died, Mom may have survived."

Marie was standing by the stove, coffee pot in hand. She put the pot down. "I can't believe what I'm hearing. I never knew you thought about Gran in that way. But then, I never really knew you. Thomas, did I? One of the things Gran tried to teach us was that life has boundaries. Guess you weren't listening." She turned and started out of the room. "Let yourself out, Thomas. I don't want to talk to you anymore today."

He called after her as she left the kitchen, "Our mother believed that Gran was pleased she was sick, that Gran wanted us to herself."

Marie left Thomas sitting at the kitchen table, grabbed her raincoat in the front closet, and walked to the corner grocery store. She didn't need anything, but she had to get away from him. She pushed a cart up and down the aisles, picking a can of this, a package of that off the shelves. Her mind was reeling with the things Thomas had said about

Gran. She was beginning to think that she had never really known her brother.

She stayed away from the house for half an hour, returned, and went in the back door with her bag of groceries. Thomas was still there. She could hear him moving around upstairs. She ran up to find him rummaging through her small bedroom desk. When she entered the room, he swung around to face her, holding up a sheet of paper.

"Found it!" he cried, and then he tore it in little bits and stuck the pieces in his jacket pocket. He rushed past her and ran down the stairs.

He was in the back porch putting on his raincoat when she caught up to him. "Thomas, do you think I would have filed that letter in my desk without making copies of it?"

He stood, his raincoat half on, staring at her. "You have a copy?" He said the four words slowly, as if she spoke a different language, and then he left.

The minute Thomas was out of the house, Marie phoned Kate's school and left a message for her. She asked Kate to meet her for lunch.

When Kate slid into the restaurant booth, she took her her sandwich and tea off the tray she was carrying before asking, "What's up?"

"Thomas came over this morning to talk." She told Kate about the visit and how it had ended.

"Kate, I'm still in shock about the way Thomas talked about Gran. I keep going over and over in my mind the way things were when we were little kids. My memories of that time are nothing like Thomas's memories." Two tears ran slowly down her face. "Kate, Thomas was such a good brother to me. Do you remember the time he made enough money shoveling snow to buy me ice skates, and then taught me how to skate? He was only twelve when he did that. And he helped me with my homework. He taught me how to dance, and how to drive a car. My God, how could he have been such a good brother, and do what he did to Jamie Campbell?"

"Marie, there's no way you're going to make sense of what's happened, and what's happened is beyond your control." Kate glanced at her watch. "I have to get back to school. Marie, I'm going to pack an overnight bag after school and move in with you. I'd just feel better if you weren't alone for the next few days."

That evening, Marie and Kate washed up the supper things, poured the last of the tea into their cups, and moved into the living room. They had just sat down when Thomas arrived. He looked freshly showered and shaved, and was wearing his favourite tweed jacket.

"I almost turned back when I saw Kate's car in the drive," he said, "but then I decided she might as well hear what I have to say. You'll be telling her anyway." He turned to Kate, "I suspect you know that I was always jealous of your friendship with Marie. I never had a friendship like that. I'm glad Marie has you, especially now."

Kate stood up. "I'll go upstairs, Thomas."

"Stay. This will only take a few minutes."

Marie had never seen fear on her brother's face, but she was seeing it that moment. She said, "Sit down, Thomas."

"I'd rather stand." He spoke directly to Marie. "It was hearing that you had made copies of Winifred's letter that made me believe that you had every intention of turning me in. I phoned Halifax divinity this afternoon. They're going to send someone to take over at St. Andrew's by the end of the month. I'm to work in the office at the College, live there, while I receive psychiatric treatment." His voice was expressionless as he said the words. He could have been giving the weather report. He paused, then turned toward the front door.

Kate got up quietly and went upstairs.

Thomas stood in the hall doorway. "Don't think I'm not suffering, Marie. Don't think I don't loathe myself. That's the ultimate punishment, you know, the self-loathing. That, and knowing that the sinning will be part of you forever, knowing that I've filled your life with such sadness. You, who were, as Gran used to say, such a bonny little soul."

Marie sat there, unable to move, saying nothing.

"And don't think that I'm not down on my knees, praying for deliverance from this perversion. Marie, I know what this must be doing to you." He came back into the room, his arms held out to her in supplication.

She held up a hand to stop him. "Please, don't, Thomas. Please."

"You're never going to forgive me, are you?"

"It isn't my forgiveness you should be seeking."

"I wish I could turn back the clock, that you had never found out."

"I've wished that myself, that I had never opened your study door that morning. I fantasized about us having our old life back. Once I opened the door and saw you, I knew that there would never be a taking back of that moment. Such secrets need to be out. Jamie needs that door opened."

He left without saying another word.

When Thomas was gone, Kate came downstairs. She

poured them each a brandy, and they sat in silence for several minutes. Marie didn't touch the brandy. "I feel as if a big stick's been shoved down my throat and is churning up my stomach." She looked at her friend. "You're crying, Kate."

"Tears of relief, my dear. I'm glad that you're not the one going to Halifax."

"How am I going to stop the obsessive thoughts in my head?"

"Time, Marie. Time."

"This morning, at the grocery store, one of the clerks was arranging the seed rack. I bought three packets of seeds. Remember how every spring Gran planted petunias in those front window boxes?" Marie went out to the kitchen, got the seeds, and showed them to Kate. "Gran liked pink, a deep rosy pink, and that's what I bought. I'm going to honour the memory of Gran's love with pink petunias."

"Wherever she is Marie, she's smiling, knowing that you did what had to be done. Come Spring, those window boxes are going to be filled with the most beautiful pink petunias in the world."

CHRISTMAS GIFTS

There were many things troubling Laura that late December day. She stood at the pantry counter, her work-worn hands kneading the huge ball of dough. It was one task that usually relaxed her. She formed the dough into loaves and set them in pans to rise. She timed the baking so that she was lifting the hot bread out of the oven just as her two girls arrived home from school, hungry and full of anticipation.

The minute they were in the kitchen, she began to slather slices of hot bread with butter and molasses as they hurried out of their coats. Laura always said a silent prayer of thanks that it was an affordable treat in hard times.

The war had just begun. She was thankful that her children were girls. Her father had served in the first world war only to be killed in the coal mine the year he returned from war. She lost her husband, Greg, to the pit a year ago and was still in mourning.

Christmas was ten days away and Laura still didn't have a gift for her mother. She had knit each of her girls a sweater, and she knew her mother was knitting them matching mittens and toques.

She knew her sister Cora's two daughters would turn up their noses at the little gifts her girls made for their Grandma.

Laura often thought about there being no males in the family. *We're a family of females. Mother, Cora and myself. Mother has two daughters and Cora and I each have two daughters. Mother and I lost our men to the pit. Cora's husband, James, died of a heart attack in his forties.*

Laura longed for her and Cora to be closer. That they weren't close was Laura's secret sorrow. She often observed her best friend, Marg, and her sister Janet together. She remember saying to Marg one time, "What wouldn't I give to have Cora treat me the way your sister Janet treats you."

Marg had given her a hug and said, "You can pretend I'm your sister."

Cora's visit that morning had added to Laura's anxiety about Christmas. She would give anything not to have to spend part of Christmas day at Cora's house, but that wasn't possible.

These days, if Laura wanted to see her mother, she had to walk down the road to Cora's house. Cora's overbearing manner made Laura feel as if she were one of the neighbours dropping by.

When their mother had a stroke some months ago, without discussing it with Laura, Cora had moved their mother from the hospital to her place. After all, Cora insisted, her house had every comfort, and plenty of room. Unspoken, was the fact that Cora's husband had been a mine manager, and left her with life insurance and a good widow's pension. She could well afford to look after her mother.

A couple of days ago, Cora had stopped in on her way home from town. "Put the kettle on, Laura. I'm exhausted from shopping. I need a cup of tea." Laura was used to her older sister's bossy ways. She put down the carrot scraper and reached for the kettle.

Over tea, Cora ticked off on her fingers the gifts she had bought that morning. When she said, "I bought mother a lovely new flannelette nightgown. It's pale blue with a bit of white lace at the collar."

Laura willed her face to remain expressionless. She excused herself and went into the pantry. She didn't want to give Cora an opening to ask her what she was giving their Mother.

When they were growing up, Laura had been the smart one, the pretty one, the popular one, and Cora, four years older had resented it.

Cora used to make sarcastic remarks about people complimenting Laura. Cora acted as if she still held a grudge even now that their lives were as different as two lives could be.

When Laura returned to the kitchen, she said, "Just checking my bread. I've set some raisin bread. The girls love it. Mother likes raisin bread too. I'll drop by with a loaf in time for supper."

"No thanks, Laura. I stopped by Shaw's bakery and bought a loaf of raisin bread for Mother."

Three days before Christmas Laura still didn't have a gift for her mother. Her meager pension allowance barely covered necessities. Cora promised to drop in Christmas Eve with a box of oranges, Christmas candy and nuts. Laura would receive the box with gratitude, and say, "You're very generous, Cora."

Cora would likely give a pleased sniff and say, "Don't mention it. I can afford to be generous."

Laura wished she could look forward to Christmas dinner at Cora's. The meal would be lavish, as would the decorations and the gifts under the tree. She berated herself for her gloomy thoughts. *I have my health, two darling healthy daughters, good friends. I believe with all my heart that things are going to get better.*

That evening, when the supper things had been put away, Ginny, twelve and the oldest, announced, "Mom, Katie and I are calling a family meeting."

"This sounds important," Laura smiled at the two dear faces looking so serious. They had family meetings on a regular basis, mostly to discuss problems and plans.

Katie, eight years old, piped up, "It's about Christmas."

Ginny said quickly, "We don't want to go to Aunt Cora's house for Christmas dinner."

"We'd rather stay home, just the three of us," Katie added.

Katie was the soft hearted one. Laura asked her, "Sweetie, what about Aunt Cora's feelings? She'll be disappointed if we don't go there for Christmas dinner."

Katie's eyes filled with tears. "Well, I don't like it at

Aunt Cora's. I want us to be together here."

"Mom, we can go to Aunt Cora's for a visit after church on Christmas Eve," Ginny suggested. Then she added, her voice full of determination, "Let's get on with this meeting."

Laura told the girls she would give their request serious thought but she couldn't promise that they would be able to turn down Aunt Cora's invitation to dinner.

The next day when the girls had left for school, Laura put on her coat and walked to town to do an errand she didn't really want to do.

She took the shortcut to town, walking along the railway tracks that ran parallel to the pit head. She tightened the soft fur collar of her dark green coat around her ears. Greg had given her the coat for Christmas two years ago, and next to the engagement ring in a small box in one of her coat pockets, it was the most precious thing she owned. Wearing the coat brought back good memories of the life she and Greg had shared.

At the pawnshop, Mr. McNeil offered her more than the ten dollars she requested. He nodded his bald head in understanding when she told him she planned to get her ring back as soon as possible. He nodded again. "I understand Misses. And don't you worry, I'll store your ring in a safe place. It'll be here when you come back for it."

From the pawnshop she went to Eaton's and bought her mother a pretty necklace of pale green beads. Her sweet, dainty mother loved pretty things. Laura couldn't remember a time that her mother didn't wear a broach, earrings, or a string of beads. Sometimes all three at the same time.

She stopped at the grocery store and bought half a

pound of chocolate maple buds as a surprise for Ginny and Katie. There was a pot of beef and barley soup simmering on the back of the stove for supper.

After supper Laura planned to place a dish of the chocolates in the centre of the table before she called her family meeting. She couldn't wait to see the look on the girls' faces when she told them that they would have Christmas dinner at home.

She wasn't looking forward to the look on her sister's face when she made the announcement that she and her girls decided to have Christmas dinner at home. Laura would deal with that another day.

That pre-Christmas family meeting held a few surprises for Laura. When she told Ginny and Katie her decision not to go to Aunt Cora's Christmas day, the two of them began giggling.

Ginny was the first one to speak. "Mom, the past few weeks Katie and I have been running errands for older people and we saved every nickel. We made enough to buy a goose or chicken for Christmas dinner."

Katie clapped her hands, "And guess what Mom! Ginny and me bought a present for you to give Grandma!"

A small box was placed in Laura's hands. Ginny said, "We know how Grandma loves earrings. We picked these out for her."

Laura thought she had kept her feelings about not having money to buy her mother a gift to herself. She opened the box and looked at the small green enameled Christmas trees.

"Grandma will love these," she said.

Some of her stowed away grief lifted as she held out her

arms to her daughters. "Your dad would be so proud of you both."

As Laura sat there, holding her daughters tightly, she knew with a sudden and sweet realization that they were going to make it. She knew that the feelings of powerlessness would lessen in time, and that she and her girls would find ways to make life work for them.